JUNK

The Back Streets of Bangkok

Scott Shaw

Buddha Rose Publications

First Printing 1989

ISBN-10: 1-877792-05-5
ISBN-13: 978-1877792052

Library of Congress Catalog Card Number: 89-81102

4 3 2 1 0 9 8 7 6 5
Printed in the United States of America

JUNK
The Back Streets of Bangkok

Table of Contents

I'm sitting here at the typing keys. It's a rainy night in L.A. A rainy day that's turned into a rainy night. One of those days that should just be forgotten. One of those days that would have been simply better not lived.

The rain whispers to me of its Zen-like perfection. It speaks to me of its profound essence.

I sit here in the space of rapidly fading intoxication, when the memory of Thailand comes to mind.

Thailand... Bangkok... where the dream reigns supreme. Where every desire is just so fucking haveable. And life, like a magician pulling a rabbit out of a hat, is filled with illusion.

Illusion yes, that's how I meet her—the girl this story is about. Illusion, she came to me in an unexpected flash of light. Revealed in light but walked me down the path of shadowed darkness—where all the sinners breed in their realms of passion. Me, I felt right at home.

Religion tells us that everything we do is sin. It makes us feel guilty for anything it doesn't find acceptable. What is sin? What is acceptable? Isn't it purely based on a definition of culture? I mean, religion promises if we're good we'll live in Heaven forever. Everyone wants to live forever, don't they? Not me. That's another fool's poison. My elixir is the temporary enlightenment that can only be found out on the outskirts, out on the hard road, in the distant realms of Asia. That's where I was introduced to her, the girl. That's where she introduced me to the goddess, *Pong kow.*

Pong kow, powder white, heroin—junk by any other name.

It's not that I'm so much for the substance. It's simply that I'm not that much against it.

Pong kow, the feeling of its intoxication is oh so sweet, like the kiss of orgasm, the touch of *shakipat*—never ending, never dying—only a moment lost into the realms of oblivion—crossing the barriers of the abyss into the land of enlightenment and freedom. The kingdom of the forgotten, where the Gods who stalk the nights in their wisdom have lost the need for any thought that anything is wrong or evil.

The powder is the goddess. It's being caressed by the perfect dream, the perfect woman—love everlasting. It's living where there is no tomorrow—for there is no need for the need for tomorrow. What is tomorrow?

The powder is all of these things—it's more. There is, however, a fine line—a very fine line; between the place where it is the master of you or you are the master of it. The master of what, I long ago realized. For in a life that exists for only the shortest of moments—where anything that one does, can be equally accomplished by another. A life where only society tells us whether we are good or bad.

Introduced by a woman—this is her story—lived on the Back Streets of Bangkok, where love, like the experience of getting high on *pong kow,* takes control of your entire being and you are never left whole, sane, or complete again. Read on...

Chapter 1

It was Thailand, more than a few years ago. I was sitting back with a female friend of mine at her small Bangkok apartment. The temperature was hot, as Thailand always promises. The evening was young—I was young.

"I thought that you might come by tonight, Stewart." Said my female friend.
"Yeah, well you know how it is, sometimes the painting gets old and the walls close in and there is nowhere to turn but out."

She ignored my rather, what I thought, profound statement.

"I thought that you may come by, so I picked up a little surprise for us."
"Yeah, I love surprises."

With this, she reaches over to her purse and pulls out a little vile of powder white—*pong kow* as it is known in Thai. Heroin by any other name…

"Yeah," I said.
"Yeah," she answered.
"Have you ever tried it?"
"Not until tonight."

We both laughed.

*   *   *

I was born and had grown up in the inner-city gutters of Los Angeles during the sixties. Drugs were not alien to me. I had consumed my first substance when I was ten. Speed, white cross, whites; amphetamine. From there it was on to reds, barbiturates. Then to marijuana, which I was amazingly quite afraid of smoking the first or second time around. Next came the drug of my generation, LSD. Propagated by Dr. Tim and all… Drugs, all tried and tested before I was ten years of age. Ten years old, that was a long time ago.

*   *   *

"So, Rosie, you're really into this stuff aren't you?"
"Yeah, but I can quit anytime. I just like the feeling and need it right now with all the changes my life has been going through."
"Sure, I understand."

The famous last words of any Junky…

*   *   *

Rosie was this more than beautiful Thai girl. Her real name was not Rosie at all but was Sarita. Though Sarita was her given name, Rosie was her chosen name and she preferred to be referred to by it; believing it very American. And, as she always wanted to go to the States and all... Thus and therefore, in this text so shall she be called, Rosie...

*   *   *

"How are we going to do this," I asked.

As intriguing as the prospect of getting high on the *pong kow* seemed, I was none too keen on the thought of a needle being placed into a vein upon my arm.

"Oh, we are going to smoke it."
"Cool."

I was obviously relieved.

With that, she pulled out a pack of her Marlboro cigarettes, removed one and began to empty what seemed to be about half of the tobacco out of it into an ashtray. Once that process was completed, she took her vile of *pong kow* and sprinkled a portion into the half-emptied cigarette. She then began to roll the cigarette back and forth between her finger and thumb to get it equally distributed.

"You want to light it up, Stewart?"
"No, you go ahead. You know I'm a healthy guy and don't smoke." I laughingly said.

She fired it up and we passed it back and forth between us as the Bangkok radio played Western rock music.

The illusion grabbed our souls and tomorrow began to hold no meaning in reality.

*　　*　　*

the first embrace
the first kiss of the night
can there ever be any tomorrow
is there ever another need

life crawls upon us
as the evening does to the day
blackening out all of the illumination

darkening sight/darkening mind
a step away from the brutality of reality

in moments
when the lost fire of the savoir is lit
and the desires of the dreams
wait to arrive

in the second before
the lifting of the veil of illusion
there is a kiss
a flash of red
in the darkness
of the night

*   *   *

I never had been a cigarette smoker, though I have done a few in times of drunken stupor. The smoke did not bother me, however. Somehow the allure of the pagan realities of the night have a way of masking the bad and the good leaving only the necessities of the experience to be felt: lived, enjoyed, and known.

I sat there as we smoked the powder white; in some ways knowing what to expect, for I had heard stories being told. I did not know, however, how much I would come on or how fast but it didn't really seem to matter.

"How does it feel going down Stewart?"
"Like heaven in a cup."
"I see you've been around." Her smiling eyes accent her words.
"Yeah, Some."

We sat there as the time and the songs on the radio progressed—we continued our consumption of the *pong kow.* She rolled the first three or four, then got up to get us a couple Singha beers to wash the taste down. By this point I was beginning to feel the movement of the perpetual illusion coming upon me. It wasn't so different from the feeling of the drug we call, 'Loads,' in L.A. And. not too different from being too drunk to know you are drunk on alcohol. You know, one of those days where you slowly drink too much beer over too long a period of time, where it just doesn't seem to affect you anymore. A kind of up down feeling, a separation from the moment into a realm, a space, that was hazy yet somehow more promisingly real than life itself.

*   *   *

the space
does it really matter
the moment
can it ever exist
the experience
moved into the lost promises of this life

a night lived
a feeling known
an embrace of something
that doesn't really matter
as nothing really does

*   *   *

As I sat there, I looked around her apartment—the feeling came over me as if I had never seen it before. Though, in fact, I had been there many times. The light green walls seemed somehow mystically new to me. The faded orange couch, which I sat upon, seems much newer than its worn condition described. The single bed, against the far wall, seemed so untouched, though it had been known by many. It all seemed so different.

Rosie's small shrine, which all good Thai Buddhist's have, in the corner to my left, seem so much more imperatively important to me. The statue of the Buddha, which Rosie was precisely placed in this shrine, seemed to move towards me. More so than it had ever done in the past. Somehow, instantly, the entire culture of Thailand was understood, known. I was no longer apart from it, but a part of it.

We slid; well actually I did first, from sitting on the couch to leaning against it on the brown carpet which covered Rosie's wooden floor. The evening progressed. We spoke the meaningless words that people who are high tend to do. She rolled a few more. I tried my hand at it. The first one became a total mess and she said,

"Just throw it away. Pong kow is so cheap here."

After a few more attempts, I was quite well versed in the process. No longer were we getting an occasional pop from a mass of the powder igniting. It was cool. It was smooth. The heroin laced tobacco permeated by being.

I sat there as we spoke, watched her eyes roll in her head. I though why didn't she have the stamina that I did, even though she was an old pro of the substance?

Me, being the kind of go all the way, take everything to the max person that I am, kept going for the production of the sweetly filled cigarettes. I never was one of those people to just have a social drink. To me, any intoxicating substance served one purpose, to get fucked up.

Time went on. Eventually, I felt my eyes join hers rolling back into my head.

The powder when smoked is not so different from the up/down effect of cocaine. The intensity of the substance lasts for a time, maybe fifteen or twenty and then it fades. The technique, as with blow, is to not let the feeling fade too far.

As we sat there speaking, she, at one point rapidly rose and headed quickly in the direction of the bathroom.

Upon coming out she proclaimed that she had to go puke. An unavoidable parody of the powder. She told me to expect it soon.

*   *   *

Rosie's story is perhaps an interesting one that probably deserves telling. Her mother was a maid to the Queen of Thailand. Yes, they still have a King and Queen; Prince, Princesses, and all. And yes, they still do have maids. In fact, virtually everyone in Thailand from the lower middle classes up have at least one maid. But, anyway, her mother was a Queen's maid. A very high position, to say the least, for a Thai woman.

Rosie's mother had come upon the position quite by accident. She had been the maid of this rather industrious Thai businessman, who apparently brought in some large American firms to the country, then known as Siam. For this achievement, and the financial capitol it produced, years later he was backed by the monarchy and politicians in one of the countries elections and won with little incident. Being in contact, and in the favor of, The Royal Family, it came to pass that one-day the Queen was in need of an additional maid. Quite coincidentally the gentleman was asked by one of the staff if he knew of any available maid servants worthy of the Queen's honor. Being quite fond of his Rosie's mother and believing that once she was in the Royal service she could reveal all kinds of governmental secrets to him, helping in his political post, he suggested her—his own number one maid. The Queen apparently found Rosie's mother quite acceptable and after she had gone through all the traditional channels of background checks and interviewing she became a maid to the Queen of Thailand.

It was quite unknown at the time, but Rosie's mother was pregnant by her former employer. Hence, the father of Rosie.

Rosie's mother was relatively young at the time she became pregnant, twenty or so. As she was not married and was living in the maid quarters of her boss's household; she, as is a very common Thai practice, was induced into periodic sexual encounters with her employer. Thus, her pregnancy.

While in the employ of the Queen, it became evident that she was pregnant. The Queen believing her to have a husband never paid it, the pregnancy, a second notion. She continued working and living in the Royal maid quarters of the Bangkok palace. When it came time to give birth, she did so, all expenses paid by the Royal Family. Never revealing that her child was illegitimate.

Upon giving birth, the Queen offered to name the baby. Which is almost a mind-boggling honor to the average Thai—to have your baby named by the Queen of Siam. Hence Rosie was born and given the name of, Sarita.

Due to her mother's relationship with the Royal Family, Rosie was educated at the best schools Bangkok had to offer. Which explains her perfect diction of the English and French languages.

Rosie never really knew her father. Her mother upon becoming aware of her condition and the man's unwillingness to accept any responsibility, claiming it was not his child and so on, never revealed any of the hoped for Royal secrets, and refused any further association with him. Which in the long run was probably best for her because he later was charged with corruption and sent to a Thai prison, which is no picnic ground.

Life was fairly good for Rosie in her early years. She lived with her grandparents and saw her mother frequently.

Her mother, unfortunately, passed away when Rosie was thirteen of some sort of a fever and though the Thai Royal Family generally were more than willing to give financial support in such cases, upon finding out the truth of who her father was, decided not to do anything further to her. Thus, the schools went out the window, the life style which she had become quite accustom to was gone, and her grandparents becoming quite old, well, she, Rosie hit the streets, becoming a lady of the evening. Life and destiny, huh?

*   *   *

Rosie leaned over close to me. I could feel that feeling sore into my heart. You know the one, where your entire being is filled with the perfection of infatuation.

*   *   *

love
the perpetual motion
love
the perpetual illusion
nothing else can even come close

real men
they never fall in love
real men
they never feel a thing
does that then make me not a real man
I feel it all
I fall in love all the time
especially with those
I should never have a feeling for

a touch of the disaster
a glance of the light
a torch of the unknown
a promised ending in an embrace
hold me/kiss me/lie to me

                    *   *   *

"Why'd you come over tonight, Stewart?"
"I don't know."

The truth being told, I had been filled with a session
of enormous lust.

"There must be a reason you came over."
"To see you. Why else? I always come to see you, don't I?"
"Yes, you do. But a lot of men come to see me."

Words that I did not need to hear.

"But am I that kind of a man?"

Her eyes were rolling in her head. She jumped up and headed
for the bathroom again. She came out, grabbed another beer
and sat back down.

"The only bad thing about pong kow is that you always barf.
Why haven't you barfed yet Stewart?"
"I don't know."

She looks at me, with distant eyes as if she was
actually interested.

"How've your paintings been coming?"
"Okay, I guess. What about you, busy, huh?"
"Yeah," she said, "But I don't want to talk about it. I want
to talk about you. Tell me about California again."
"Okay, but first roll up another one of those bad pups. I have
to go hit the head."
"Oh, do you have to barf."
"No, I have to hang one. You know, those damn beers and
all."

I went into the bathroom. Funny Thailand is never really clean. I don't know what it is. Maybe it is just that I am from the States. But no matter where you go: the walls, the fixtures, just have this dirty feeling about them.

I drained my lizard then stood there checking my look in the mirror—fixed my hair a bit, stared deeply into my own eyes to see the condition of dilation—see what condition my condition was in.

As I stood there intoxicatedly staring into my own eyes, I remembered back to a time when I was young boy, maybe seven or eight. I was at this Methodist Sunday School as all good Protestant boys were raised to attend. The Sunday school teacher, a Japanese lady, was asking all those in attendance what parts of their body that they could see. Each kid gave out his or her answer, each answer being written down upon the chalkboard. Except those that were incorrect, of course. Me, when asked what part of my body I could see, said, *"Eyes, I can see my eyes"* She said, *"Yes,"* and wrote it on the board. At the second I said it, I realized how could I see my eyes. Then I wondered why she had written it down. I was almost embarrassed.

There was this phenomenon that I could produce when I was a child. I remember it so vividly, it's all so clear. I could be sitting playing with my toys, playing outside, doing anything—at any moment of my choice I could simply view myself, as if I were another person standing over me watching my every action. I could see myself as through the eyes of someone else. I don't know, maybe the Sunday school teacher and I had a psychic connection. Perhaps her ethereal mind instantly understood what I had meant when I had said, *"Eyes."* Perhaps, I do not know...

Anyway, back to the story at hand. I came out of the bathroom and sat back down close to Rosie. She had fired up another pathway to the abyss.

I studied her, she was so beautiful. Her skin so golden. Her hair, long, black, soft. Her eyes that kissed me every time I looked into them. I love her again—now, as I write these words. That feeling, that emotion, that touch, the heart rush—Love...

It was so sad, I thought to myself as we sat there on her floor, my arm placed around her: so beautiful, so special; and society had led her to a life on the streets—getting dicked for a dollar or a Thai *Bhat,* as it were.

It paid for her to keep up a fairly decent lifestyle, I guess, though not as grand as that of some hookers I have known in Hong Kong, Tokyo, or L.A. It kept her from living in one of those funky shacks on the river. It kept her clothed in the finest Bangkok had to offer. But, mostly, it kept her empty, not knowing how to love, who to love. It kept her from knowing who loved her. Life based in a world dominated by the ejaculation of the penis. I too was a fool haunted by the faults of destiny just like her.

*   *   *

I had returned to Thailand on my merger remaining finances. Though I had been there many times before, I had never actually lived there. I had returned at a time in my late twenties when my life, as the life of a mystic artist often does, had become quite unliveable in L.A. I had no job, no babe, and just the continual problems of the world to content with. I had come back to Thailand to paint, write, live in a world where living is easy for a Westerner. A world where illusion awaits around every corner and any dream is just a heartbeat away. I had come to Thailand to create. Instead, I found Rosie.

We had met, I guess, two months before. Rosie was a friend of a French girl I knew who had grown up in Bangkok. She was a fan of the *pong kow,* as well. We had taxied on over to Rosie's apartment one day to pick up the substance. We had gone up the stairs, two flights. The kind where you switch back at a half way interval. The building was old and dirty. I questioned my friend as to what kind of a dealer would live in such a place. My previous experiences having been with the dealers in the maximum dollar category—L.A. way. She was no dealer; it was explained, simply a friend lending a helping hand.

We knocked at the door, it was answered. There she was this goddess among women. There she was Rosie.

We went inside. I was more than taken with Rosie. Taken with her beauty, her eyes, and the prospect of love in the lust degree. Having spent the last several months with my dick in my hand, my hormones were rushing.

The transaction was completed and after brief casual talk we headed for the door, ten minutes or so after our arrival. As we walked down the stairs, my tongue dragging behind me, the obvious questions were asked on my part.

"Who is that girl?"
"Do you think she's pretty?"
"Gorgeous."
"You can do better than that. This is Bangkok."
"Maybe I don't want to do better than that."

I was then informed as to Rosie's fate in life and chosen profession of the night. I couldn't help myself though, over the next few days, I couldn't get her out of my mind. You know how the mind of desire is and all. You see it, you want it, and you got to have it.

I spoke to my French friend—oh, by the way her name is Patricia, a few days later and asked if it would be inappropriate if I were to contact Rosie. She laughed, and I was assured, in Rosie's line of work, it would be more inappropriate if I didn't contact her.

I could feel in the tone of her voice that there was more than a partial bit of jealousy on Patricia's part towards Rosie. Why, I didn't know. Though my Patricia was a bit over weight, she was, none-the-less more than beautiful. But anyway, back to the story at hand...

I was told that Rosie didn't have a telephone and that I must either find her at this one Disco she frequents, in search of prey, or must go directly to her door. Being the love to dance sort of guy that I am, I elected to go to the disco. Much to my dismay, she was not there the two evenings that I attended in pursuit of her LOVE. I however, was more than fortunate in my conquest(s) and both nights I attended I strolled home to my apartment with a more than interesting object of desire.

The first was this very so-so thirtyish accountant. Thai college educated and all but undoubtedly seeking a passport to the U.S.; as a good percentage of Thai babes are. It was *no-where's-ville* for me *Daddy-0.* I had just set up shop in Bangkok and was in no mood for the type of, *"Let's get married immediately,"* relationships that I had experienced in Bangkok in the past. Especially, when the bitch had a flat tire in the central region, virtually no pubs or boobs, and just did not known how to fuck. You know the style, even when you roll them on top, they giggle and roll back over expecting you to do all the work...

The second sweet young miss was this more than beautiful Thai of Chinese descent, very light skinned, who dressed sixties style and could she dance. (Something I must state Thais are not experts in.) We definitely, *Tripped the Light Fantastic,* her and I together.

She was young, lusty, and she could fuck. In brief, I get her back to my crib. I only turned one light on—keep it dim. She danced around still hyped on the movement from the club. She dances over to me, places a few glancing kisses upon my face. I smile, she smiles. I move over and take her in my arms—slow dance style. Our bodies move together, in the rhythm of the silence—the stereo was not on. I lean down; our lips found each other's. I lick hers; she smiles. Obviously never having been with an American dude before, she really didn't know how to play the moves of love. But, none-the-less...

We continue to move to our own inner rhythm, our kisses become more intense—tongue slapping tongue. I slide my hand down the side of her leg, bringing it up between her crouch—let my fingers do the walking. Mr. Hand moves up, then down, inside her black bell-bottomed pants. Her juices of love were flowing.

I danced her over to the couch. My couch, it was blue, fading into the black of the night. I lay her down upon it. My hand remained in place, my fingers *move'n* and *grove'n*. I pulled up from her body, looked deeply into her half-closed eyes. She smiled. I begin to unfasten her pants. You know, one of those hell sessions, with the clasp and the zipper in the back.

Man, I was up, hard, ready. I wanted to fuck. I was about to just rip them off, when she laughed and begin to help me.

She pulled her pants off, leaving her floral underwear on. Why do chicks always do that? I looked at her, halfway smiled, you know the kind, when you're not one hundred present sure if you're going to get the pussy or not.

With two hands I went for the underwear. She holds them in place. Fuck! Okay, let's play the game.

I kiss her some more, reach under her shirt. Touch her small, firm boobs. As I do that with my right hand, my left hand is haphazardly unfastening my belt, and pulling down my zipper.

We kiss, I fondle, Pants down, I roll on top, pull her underwear to one side, and plant the bad pupster home.

She was wet. It wasn't hard. She gave a little sign on the side. I drove deeper.

You know, I've said this before in poetry, but there is just something about the Southeast Asian love, maybe it's the heat, maybe it's the longitude combined with the latitude, maybe it's the dawning of the age of Aquarius, I don't know, but Dick he is always just way hard, way firm, full on triple XXX maximum forward thrust power.

This girl was tight. Dick was masterfully at full mast. He whammed hard against her upper wall.

I would have like to have a more adventurous fuck session. But, she was way into me and moved and grooved under me, with the flowing virtuosity of a master; she came maybe five minutes in. Which isn't bad, but...

So, post putting in the necessarily time requirements in to make myself feel like a man, I blew my cookies. We lay there for a while, half arched upon my couch. Occasionally kissing, veering between looking at each other and looking deeply into the night for the answer to reality. I stare into space, thinking, I could have gone for her. But, always a but... She couldn't speak English. My Thai was basic at best and I was just not in the mood for another of those carry a dictionary everywhere relationships, as experienced many-a-time in the past. So, that night was that night. Never even really saw her body. What was her name?

With my dick out of hock and my movement rekindled, it did cross my mind to chill back on the idea of moving for and towards Rosie and just forget the whole thing altogether. Yet, somehow the desire did not die. I remember thinking at the time, how I knew myself and how I always chased after illusions—always something different, always something new, and perhaps this was the same. But, a desire lived is a desire earned. So, I decided to go for it and head on over to her crib.

I approached from the West. It was early evening; being fashionably late, within its own right, as I could possibly be arriving unannounced.

I felt all those initial reservations, that doubt, *"Should I go for it or not?"* Those traditional butterflies in the stomach. It took all that I had to get myself to actually go in and up the stairs, after I had walked past the building three or four times before making my move. Then, post my assent up the stairs; it took me several minutes before I actually brought myself to knock on her door.

*   *   *

in the dream of desire
always hidden is the question

in the passage of knowledge
there always remains a feeling of sorrow

known is known
it may never be alien
never, new again

in the memories of what has been felt
there can never be the wonder of what is to come

look to the wind
and there is mystery
look to the ocean
and there is wonder
look to the rain
and the unknown answers may sound their chord
but look into the eyes of a woman
and it is the same song
sung in a different tongue

*   *   *

I knocked. It took some time before she answered. She, Rosie came to the door but her mind—her body were otherwise engaged.

"Hi Stewart, what are you doing here?"
"Oh, you remember my name?"

"Sure, I remember your name."
"I'm glad you remember my name."

She smiled. Her eyes pierced my soul.

As she held a white bed sheet around her and peered around the door, her golden skin shined and one of her very small, very perfect, very beautiful breasts was partially exposed; inviting but currently, shall I say, involved.

*   *   *

Love and knowledge
Lust and love
Business all the same
Attraction/distraction

A kiss that leads on
on to nowhere/everywhere in particular

*   *   *

Lost in the awkwardness of that moment, I knew I had nothing to say which had not been said to her before.

For a second, before my thinking mind rationalized the situation, I hoped, I thought, I dreamed that she might have been awaiting me. Then, I heard the movement, felt the presence of another life form with less than love on his mind.

"So, what's going on, Stewart?"
"Oh nothing, I guess... Just thought I'd stop by see how you are."
"Kind of busy right now."
"Yeah, I understand."
"Hey, do you have a phone, Stewart?"
"Yeah."

"I don't, I hate to be bothered by them. But, give me your number and I will call you."

So, I consciously and precisely wrote down my telephone number on one of the pages of the portable notebooks I always carry in my pocket; tore it out and gave it to her. I don't remember quite how I felt at the time. All I can seem to focus on was this confusion—probably macho in nature.

I always have a problem understanding how the world does not revolve simply around me. I always wonder how a babe, once I am in sight does not fall hopelessly in love with me. I guess that is one of my illusions, for I generally fall hopelessly in love with them.

I hit on out to the street and decided to walk home. Rosie's apartment was, in fact, not so far from mine. It was located just off of a major Bangkok street, Rama IV Road.

I walked out. The heat was hot. It seemed to become hotter as I walked. Perhaps I was over dressed for a Bangkok walk, with a sport coat on and all. But that's the way I always dress, why change just because I'm in Southeast Asia. The sweat moved its way into/onto me. Reminding me of where I was, why I was, who I was. I knew the answer to all of those questions quite well.

For any illusion is better than no illusion. And, any dream will do. If there was one thing Bangkok did have to offer—it was illusion.

I walked and was confronted by the basic pavement princesses, professing truth and immortality in a pagan night. I turned them down and walked on further. I decided to forego returning to my apartment alone. Alone, with nothing but the fumes of oil paint thinner, and turpentine to breath. I don't believe my nose and or sense of smell has ever recovered from that period of time.

I decide to go out. I was out, but out of out. Out is something I have always done so well. Escapism, I am an expert in the field. Tomorrow, later, and all that the two entail. It seems I am forever finding a reason not to do this, not to do that—not to paint, not to write, not to compose.

The outside calls with its addiction and I am under the grasp of its spell. Outside, not alone.

Promises, they are all made outside. Dreams, that is where they all are found. Everything is outside; everything is outside but inside.

I debated as to whether or not to go to the disco I had been more than lucky at the previous few nights, but elected to hit a little pizza place, cafe, I knew and get my grub on. Mostly, I didn't really want to run into the go nowhere babe situations from the night(s) before.

Chapter 2

My ego was somehow damaged in the process of the evening's plight and a dream would have been an appropriate answer—a dream in the form of female skin. Nothing came, as it never seems to do in moments as those lived that evening—those when you really need to be saved but no cavalry to the rescue.

With paper money a bit tight and no female sex slaves excepting plastic, I headed home. And though I was approached by a hooker or two, a taxi driving Pimp or three, and a guy at the door of here or there. Alone, I wallowed into my apartment. I grabbed a few brews and with hormones rushing went into and took a shower basically with the intention of choking the chicken with thoughts of what might have been. But, I just let the water flow over my desirous body—got out and went to bed dripping wet.

Next A.M., I found myself waiting, wanting Rosie to call. One of those days that you intentionally remain in the *abode de amour:* waiting, wanting, dreaming for the telephone to ring. Then, if it does, you pretend that you are so cool and busy but just happened to be home.

It never did, however, ring that is. But as I hold a basic nihilistic philosophy to life anyway, well it all just seemed right. Right in the lack of useless unrighteousness, I guess.

Though I knew of Rosie's profession—her way of life—somehow, I found myself incessantly attracted to her. It was probably my generally self-destructive nature but I wanted to know her more. I was obsessing, big time.

It was not until two days later that my telephone rang, Rosie on the other end of the line. It was early, seven in the morning. I am one who generally doesn't go to sleep until: three, four, five in the AM. So, the call was a bit of a rude awakening.

"Did I wake you Stewart?"
"Yes, but that's Okay."
"Do you know who this is?"
"Of course."
"Want to come and have breakfast with me?"
"Sure. Where?"
"How about the coffee shop at the Tawana Hotel?"
*"I don't really like it there. The food isn't very good and I
used to stay at that hotel when I first started coming to
Bangkok. It's a little dirty, don't you think?"*
"Okay, then where?"

      I lay there realizing that I was being a bit of a whiny
bitch and decided the best thing to do was just to meet her
there.

*"No that's Okay, I'll meet you there in about a half an
hour."*

      A half an hour being a joke for the traffic congestion
of Bangkok and having to drag myself out of the sack-jack
and all.

"I'd rather go somewhere that you want to be."
"No, no, really, that place is fine. See you in a little while."

      Desire fulfilled—pleasure for any fool getting what
is wanted—wrapped in human form.

*   *   *

and when there is no direction known
where can you really go
to the center of the desire

crave it

and it shall be answered

want it
and it shall be had

so let it be written
so let it be known

*   *   *

I immediately got out of bed and skipped the morning shower. I laughed to myself as I thought of the location of this hotel, for it is just off of the Pat Pong, Bangkok's red-light district. Then it dawned on me, I wonder why she is calling me so early? She must have been working all night.

The morning was right though, the desire was right. It was all being placed neatly in the palm of my hand. It's like the previous waiting is instantaneously forgotten, you know, when the love is put into full on motion.

I dressed in full ego garb. The egotism that comes with a newly found babe calling you and waking you in the morning—the morning of love.

Desire is a pagan warrior. It holds the kiss of death.

It was almost funny as I look back now, being excited over a woman calling me: a woman of the evening, a woman that so many had before, and that so many have had since. A woman, a dream, my dream, an unknown love, unknown to me, but none the less...

As I walked hurriedly down the stairs of my apartment building, the thought came to me, I could have just bought her services for the evening, then all the waiting, all the dreams would have already been fulfilled.

Luck, destiny, had its way—there was an empty *Tuk Tuk*, (the little three wheeled Bangkok taxis), going by. I hailed it and got in and got to the destination. Amazingly, the entire waking, getting dressed, and travel sojourn took only about thirty-five minutes. The *Tuk Tuk* let me off in front of the restaurant and as I looked in the large glass windows, Rosie was nowhere to be seen.

Once inside, I was accosted by the hostess as to the number to be seated. I told her that I was looking for this young lady and described her. I was informed there was no one fitting that description as of yet in the coffee shop. She seated me. I waited.

I sat there, antsy, more than a bit unhappy and wondering what kind of game was going down. Had she met a trick? Where did she call me from, etc. etc. All those games that the mind does, when conquest is in the works.

The hostess had seated me at a nice table by the window though. I ordered up a cup of the Java and watched the Bangkok scene pass by.

As one looks out onto the city: it's crowded, polluted. This day it looked almost to be permeated by an orange hue. The people that were on the streets range from the peasant poor, to the multi-millionaires, and everywhere in between. There are old cars, new cars, Rolls Royces, and even a passing hand pulled cart or two. Bangkok, though there may well be other places like it; somehow, some way. It has offered me more dreams, more illusions than any other city on Earth has even come close to.

Five minutes, ten minutes later, still no Rosie. I began to become a bit pissed, having been woken up and all. After about twenty of sitting and waiting I finally ordered up some eggs, some toast, and some of these square looking potatoes that they choose to believe are hash browns.

As the food arrived, the waitress had to make the comment, *"Isn't your friend coming?"* Which pissed me off even more. But, I played it cool and laughed off the question.

The eggs were runny, as I remembered that they had been before. I hate runny eggs. To be quite honest I don't really like eggs at all.

The potatoes, pseudo hash browns, were greasy. The meal just intensified my annoyance at the situation.

I am generally a very patient and accepting person. Somehow in the desire of this moment, the lack of sleep, my blood sugar being off, and eating lousy food that did not please my pallet, I was kick'n annoyed.

*   *   *

the wait—for the meal of destiny
the wait—for the love intertwined

love intertwined
love in mind
lust by any other name

the kiss of obscurity
the kiss of the unknown
forever longing
forever sought
forever is forever
forever—it never goes away

*   *   *

I sat there just having finished my plate of poison. I sat there staring out onto the Bangkok abyss feeling less than happy, drinking a final cup of coffee, and then I was going to bail. Then, there, out of nowhere, she walked in, or should I say danced into the room. She passed by the hostess virtually ignoring her. What style. Her eyes caught mine and all the anger was gone.

She wore this flowing black dress, (the best whores only wear black), and deep red lipstick. Her high heels melodically embraced the floor, pronouncing her movement across it. Her image, her vision, she took control of my soul.

I was her slave, her servant, no mind of my own. Why did I ever need a soul, when creatures such as her roamed the face of the earth?

*   *   *

embraced without a word
no word that may be spoken

touched without a movement
no movement that may be seen

loved without a notion
no notion of what it had to offer

and the builders build
and the Gods tear down
but the walls they are all the same

into the realm of the unforgiving
I was lost in her grasp
I have never been able to find myself since that day
lost forever more

*   *   *

As she approached, I stood up and she moved right up to me and placed one upon my lips.

"Waiting long Stewart?"
"No, not too long at all. I had breakfast though."
"Oh, how could you. I'm so hungry."
"Eat, please. You know me, I've got no place to be."
"No place?"
"No place."

She signalled the waitress and ordered her meal. I sat there stunned by her beauty.

"What do you do Stewart, do you have a job?"
"A job! No, no job. I'm an artist."
"An artist? I'd love to see your work. Can you paint me?"
"I have been painting pictures of you ever since I began painting."
"Painting pictures of me? But we just met?"
"But I've dreamed of you, forever."
"Oh, you think I am beautiful?"
"To say the least."
"Yes, men always tell me I am beautiful."

Suddenly, I was grounded. My feet abruptly smashed upon the floor.

Perhaps, at that moment, I should have seen what was to come. For in that moment it was revealed to me who she really was, in all of her disheartening unrealistic glory. For a second, I had forgotten. And perhaps unfortunately, I was soon to forget it again.

Her breakfast came. I had another few cups of Java, sliced up in my direction. She ate. I watched her eat, though I pretended to do otherwise.

"What do you do all day, Stewart?"
"Sleep! Bangkok is too fucking hot during the day to do anything else."
"Do you have air conditioned?"
"Yeah, or I wouldn't be able to sleep in the daytime."
"I love air conditioning; my apartment doesn't have it. Let's go to your place before it gets too hot."

I was almost dumbfounded for a moment. Was it all that easy? I tried to remind myself that she was just a hooker but somehow it all seemed, felt so different. For it wasn't as if I had picked her up off the street or met her in the proverbial palaces of the night—as one generally does in the usual case of a whore. It was more as if I had met her and was going after her like a seize-and-conquest type of typical male female relationship thing.

I believe it was at this point when I lost all perspective on the relationship. The relationship: hers and mine.

We got the bills, two separate checks, for hers was ordered separately. She handed her bill to me without even a second thought, in all the perfection and poetry of the perfect whore. I paid them, as I would have done anyway. Being the perfect gentleman that I am.

Outside into the heat we went. Hit like a tidal wave, like a tsunami in the depths of the darkest nightmare; awoke to the plain, hard, and painful facts of the day at hand. I wish I could say it was sweet. It was not. The air was polluted, and hot, too hot.

"Do you have a car Stewart?"
"Not in Bangkok. Do you?"
"I don't know how to drive. How will we get to your apartment?"
"Taxi, I guess."
"Good, I am glad you didn't say Tuk Tuk. I hate Tuk Tuk."
"I think they are kind of fun."
"That is because you are a Westerner. By the way what country are you from?"
"America."

I then properly saluted.

I noticed her eyes light up, just a bit at the mention of the name. She obviously had a fascination with the good old U.S. of A.

"Have you ever been there?"

"No, but I want to go very much."

"Here we go again," I thought. *"A green card in one eye, a dollar sign in the other."* Why can't people in Thailand just see me for who I am, take the time to know me, or at least check out my hairstyle or the clothing that I wear. No, all they see is a Westerner and when they hear American, the rest is history. It's instantaneous love in the works.

But then, I realized, I guess that's why I was there, who was I fooling; instant and easy love.

We hailed a taxi with little problem and were on the road again. The taxi was one of the better ones, air-co complete.

As we sat down and the drive began, she moved closer and took my hand; holding it softly, gentle. The silent caress of the perfect goddess—unknown to man, until this, the moment of origin. We spoke of the usual get to know one another things and the ride went along easily enough, with just a touch of impending lust.

Out of the taxi we stepped, re-emerged into the heat of the forming Bangkok day. We made our way forward into my building—up the stairs to the third floor, the top floor. The top floor, a requirement of mine; for I had become so sick of having footsteps and noise above me in my place back L.A. way. I unlocked the door and moved once again into the cool air space within the walls of air-conditioned comfort.

"What's that smell?"
"Oil paints, turpentine, and thinners."
"What?"
"Painting stuff."

My Bangkok apartment was nice by most standards; expensive by all standards—mostly due to the fact that there was very little street noise—very unusual in Bangkok. It was a large, modern, one bedroom. I used the bedroom for creating and lived predominantly in the living room. My bed, couch, and the rest of the things were well placed and arranged in the room. The apartment, in the overall picture, was a mess, of course. I was way too touchy about my possessions to have a maid and I have never been able to find the time, with creativity and all, to keep my living spaces ship shape.

At that introductory moment, however, I was almost ashamed of the mess: the dirty clothes, books, journals, and all, that so randomly occupied the space.

"I want to see one of your painting."
"Let's go."

As we passed the bed *en route* to my studio in the bedroom, Rosie's hand so softly moved over the metal footboard.

"Nice bed."

Into the studio area; there were several paintings which I had finished and were leaning against the wall and others still drying hanging on three of the four walls.

"This is your art?"
"Yeah, do you like it?"
"It looks like a child's art. I could do that."
"Why don't you then?"
"I don't know?"
"That's the difference between an artist and the average person, the artist does it, the average person finds excuses not to."
"But this is so simple."
"Simplicity is truth."
"Yeah, but..."

"There are no buts. Haven't you ever seen Neo-expressionistic art before?"
"Neo, what? Do you get money for this?"
"No, that would make me a business man."
"I can see why. Anybody could do this."
"Look, I'm not going to argue this point with you for you obviously have never developed an eye for art. Each piece is its own reality. It creates itself. I may have ideas but they are only the basis. Each color is formed into its own perfection. It then merges with the next, all in their own perfection forming the painting. Letting it create itself."
"I've seen stuff like this in movies but I like landscapes and portraits."
"This one here is a portrait."
"But it doesn't look real."
"Landscapes and that lousy typical portrait art you speak of, a camera can do that much better. This is feeling!"
"Well maybe. I like that one over there."

She points to a nude hanging on the wall.

"Let's go listen to some music."

She leads me out of the room.
I had heard all these kind of ridiculous comments before, from all the people who had never opened their eyes. Somehow though, maybe it was my lack of sleep, but I was just in no mood for amateur criticism this day.

"Nice bed."

She reiterated while running her hand along the footboard once again as we re-entered my main living space.

"Have a seat. Would you like something to drink?"
"Do you have whiskey?"

Ah, a person after my own heart; intoxication at 10:00 A.M.

"No, actually I don't. I got rather too blasted on it a few years back and haven't been unable to drink it since."
"That's because you didn't drink it again the next day."
"I had a hangover for a week. I thought I definitely cracked a piston on that one. I've got some beer and vodka though."
"Well Stewart, I guess you will just have to give me a drink of both."

I laughed.

"How would you like your vodka?"
"Why, in a glass please."

She was obviously trying to be humorous.

"With orange juice, or my preference of poison, with grapefruit juice."
"Straight please."
"Okay."

I love the people who know how to dance.
Into the kitchen I went. I soon realized that the movement of motion was at hand and she had followed me in. As I was grabbing the bottles of brew from the refrigerator and two beer mugs and the vodka out of the freezer, she came up close to me, next to me. She leaned against me, while looking around my shoulder in the refrigerator,

"What do you have in there?"
"Virtually nothing as you can see."

I sliced my way past her, oh so amorously, and leaned against the counter.

Next to me again, she asks,

"What do you have in there?"

As she puts her finger in and pulls back the top of my pants. I smile.

It was obvious; she was obvious—almost too obvious. Too obvious like a cheap whore—like a slut without a dick between her legs. Too obvious like all the women, unmarried women who have the emptiness in their eyes, who desperately seek a man to fill that emptiness. Empty until their eyes find that all the dreams proved to be lies and were oh so unfulfilling.

I do not like the obvious. It is never what it seems.

We went back to living room, both of us with two drinks in hand: a beer and a vodka.

Upon the couch she sat and kicked off her high-heeled shoes. She crossed her legs, revealing a run in her black stocking.

She smiled. She one sipped her vodka. Set the beer on the floor.

"I'm tired Stewart. Are you tired? Let's take a nap."

I was tired too, no doubt. Somehow the embrace of the day had awakened me though: the sun, the heat, the wait, the Thai coffee, a babe of babes with her high heels off and a run in her black stockings.

Before I could say yes, no, or maybe, Rosie had stood up and was unzipping her dress and beginning to remove it. Thai's, are not known for their subtleties.

As she slipped it off, the radiance of her body was beginning to reveal itself. She had a black, almost see through bra on, and black, I believe they are called, panty hose. Underwear, no. No underwear to speak of. Her panty hose and their shape, design, and form, revealing and almost blending into her perfectly formed black pubic hairs.

I always have been a pussy man. Some dudes dig the legs or the boobs. Me, it's the sight of the zone of conquest, the basis for all humanity; the beaver that gets me aroused.

I sat there, shall I say, a bit mesmerized. I had nothing to say. What could say?

She removed her bra, exposing the beautifully formed small breasts, which I had a glimpse of two or three nights the previous. She sat on the bed, preciously, articulately removing her panty hose. Then, she threw them over on my chair. She stood up, looked at me, smiled, spun around one time on her toes with the perfection of a prima ballerina, a dervish, and asked,

"Do you like what you see?"

She then jumped, literally jumped on to my bed; laughing, pulling the covers over her,

"Nice bed," she laughingly exclaimed.
"It was made in Italy," I said.

*   *   *

doubt fades to wisdom
wisdom is left to intellectual remains
knowledge becomes the abstract concept
desire the key to it all

illusion merges with the embracing of desire
desire, can it ever be cured
known, maybe
felt, for sure
cured, I don't think so

just moved from one form onto the next

*   *   *

She lay there giggling. I hit my vodka, but I must admit, not as eloquently as she. I kicked off my shoes, stood up unbuttoned my shirt, took off my pants. Not to be out done, spun around,

"Do you like what you see?"
"I love it."

I climbed into bed. Before I could even really get in she was pushing her way next to me. Her body felt warm, intense. It must be the heat of her Thai blood, I thought.

"I love air conditioning Stewart, because you can get cold and snuggle up tight. You said you are American, does it get cold in America?"
"I'm not really American, I'm Californian. It's different, you know."
"Oh, I have heard of California. It's hot like Bangkok, yes?"
"Not really, it's a lot cooler. The winters are the best."
"Will you take me to California, Stewart?"
"Of course, let's go tomorrow."

My standard answer to the standard Asian female question.

"Really?"
"Really."

She kissed me—she kissed me again.
My words could never, can never describe the poetry of the first embrace, the first kiss. I can only place it in literary prose and blatant descriptions in hopes that any clear

imagination may find a way to understanding the overwhelming totality of it. I'll leave its definition to the attempts of other writers of other times.

I lay on my side, she on hers. As her arms embraced my body I lost the conception of what was real, what was definable. My heart pounded with the love. Her embrace was devastating.

After several kisses she, took hold of my love toy. It was already hard. Full-on hard. She stroked it once or twice. She rolled herself on top of me. As she did, I could feel her wet vaginal canal leaking slowly onto my leg.

There had apparently been enough foreplay for her. Me too, I was up, I was hard. I was ready. With my dick still in her hand, she took it and placed it between her legs: inserted it deeply, directly. It didn't all fit. My head hit hard against her upper wall. She didn't care, with a slight, *"Oooh,"* she continued, she made love to me, as opposed to my making love to her.

She moved slowly, cautiously, perfectly on the topside, rocking and rolling back and forth. She knew what she was doing—I guess that is logical, I mean, you know, she did have the practice. She moved and grooved. I softly rubbed her breasts. It was like the perfect fit, the perfect love, the perfection of the universe—Tantric enlightenment. Submerged in the moment, nothing else mattered.

Most whores are of the type: do the job, fuck 'em, get 'em to cum, get it over with, and out. This was different, very different. She moved slowly on the top, Dick deeply in her, massaging her clitoris upon my body—eyes closed—as lost in the moment as I was. She came, really came. I took hold of her hips, drove my dick in deeper, forcefully controlled her upward action movements upon me. I made her, make me cum.

We had completed our rolls. She fell off me, fulfilled. She moved in close to me. We lay there bound within each other's embrace.

Though it was more than perfect, more than beautiful, my mind wondered to the fact that there I was, having just fucked—made love, to a prostitute. She had obviously been out all night. How many had known her love? How many diseases had entered her body? How many men were filled with the same feeling of ecstasy and infatuation that I was? It, the feeling, made me pull from her embrace and roll over.

Rosie, rolling with me, holding on from behind said,

"Do you know what I do Stewart?"
"Yes, but it doesn't matter?"

An answer, but not the truth.

"Do you know how many man I have known."
"No, do you?"
"No."
"Really, I don't want to talk about this," I bluntly said.
"Okay, but I want you to know that I make them all wear rubbers."

Saying this—my mind in the disease category, was put partially to rest.

"Why didn't you make me wear one?"
"Because I want to have your baby."

"Fuck," I thought. What a game, what a dance. Who was setting the rules to it anyway? I didn't know. The last thing I wanted was to bring a child into this world of desire, this world of pain. What the fuck was going on? Was it her way to get me to marry her? Well, the joke was on her, for if that was the case, there was no way in the world that I would just because of her being knocked up. Was it her way to get to the States? Or was it just something she said to all her

men, like I promise all the women matrimony. I was again worried of disease. I was again unhappy and confused, and I did not feel like sleeping.

Rosie had already, almost instantaneously, fallen asleep after her last words. I lay there dazed—thinking too much as I tend to do. Finally, after about a half an hour or so, I too feel asleep.

It was about three in the afternoon when I woke up. I believe it was due to the soft sweet snoring Rosie was performing in my left ear. I woke and thought I was in the mood for love, if you know what I mean. Dick was hard. But, I rose quietly after analysing my current situation. I went and hit the showers, hoping Rosie may hear it and join me. There was no response to that desire, however. I finished, dried off, grabbed a brew, and decided to paint.

Now, I'm of the artistic nature to finish a painting in one sitting. It's rare, very rare, that I ever work on the same painting day after day. I feel that by creating art in this fashion the expression is organic, less contrived. Also, due to this creative process, I'm left with an enormous amount of paintings I don't like. Not like those artists who work and work until all is of the desired quality. But even the bad and the mediocre paintings have their essence in this technique of expression—perfection with in imperfection, the key to the universe.

I only tell you this to better explain the situation of that moment; Rosie's and mine... She was sleeping. I was not. She was in my apartment/painting studio, so was I. My stretched, upon, stretcher bars of canvas were all painted upon. Thus, I was left with only two options; that is if I choose to go ahead with the idea of painting—one, I had to cut canvas from the roll and stretch it onto wooden bars and staple gun it, in place; or two, the second option was to simply cut and staple a length of canvas to the wall; which would only take like three or four hits of the staple gun as opposed to several. After considerable thought, it is amazing how the mind loves to find its folly, I decided to just put some canvas on the wall.

I have to admit it did annoy me a bit, the unnecessary consideration I had to pay another person and all. I mean this is why I lived alone: for space, for freedom. Perhaps it was simply my mind and the fact that I wish the entire universe to revolve around me. And, I wanted Rosie to have awakened when I did—but she had not. Anyway... I began to paint.

The paint began to move itself upon the canvas; golden brown in color in the perpetual shape and form of Rosie's made love to body, now laying upon my bed. I painted, the time ticked. How long, I do not know.

As I painted, Rosie entered the room in all her nudity and placed her arms around my neck from the rear hugging me.

"What are you doing Stewart?"

Without a hesitation in the brushes movement,

"Painting of course."
"Come take a shower with me."
"I already did. Didn't you hear me?"
"How could I? I was sleeping. Please take one with me."
"I'm painting."
"You must. I will not take no for an answer."

With this, she began to drag me by my arm into the bathroom and literally rip off my special painting clothes. In the shower we were.

Now, I don't know if other men have this little situation happen to them or not but I, especially when it's with a new sweet young thing in my presence and I have not just blown my rocks, I have the tendency to get a hard-on when the ritual two-some shower is taking place. It's like,

"Stay down, think of something else, come on, STAY DOWN!" But when slobs are being laid on you and the water is warm and sensual, all the body lecturing in the world does nothing to keep the sword of Gideon sheathed.

She was all over me—what could I do. I gave her the special soap up both of our bodies and rub them together, let's get lusty treatment. Lusty it was. Some girls who are tall enough, I can make love to them standing up in the shower. Others they can turn around and lean against the shower wall and I can bend my knees a little and let the power pup enter from behind. Allowing them to cop a plea of ecstasy in that direction. Rosie, undoubtedly, well trained in all the methods of Thai eroticism, (there is few cultures of the twentieth century where it has flourished more), she climbed her way up and standing on the bathtub ledge, she slid her wet beaver over my erected dick.

She put her arms around my neck, held on. Her lips locked onto mine. She let her knees and legs take control of the action—she moved back and forth, up and down on my element of love.

It went on for a while, the sex, that is. She held tighter and tighter, breathing harder and harder. The water ran down over our bodies, washing away all thoughts of sin.

She finally pulled her lips away from mine as she came. Her feet dropped to the floor of the tub. She held on to me. She was done, I was not.

She kissed me.

"You didn't cum, Stewart?"
"No."
"Why?"

Without an answer, I turn her around, planning to perform the aforementioned enter the beaver from behind love play. She seemingly knew what was happening. She put her hands against the shower wall. I moved into position.

She reached back, took a hold of my dick, rubbed it so gently along the outside of her pussy. I thought she was just searching for the hole. Then, she lifts up on her toes, takes my dick, and begins to put it in her ass.

"You'll have to be gentle, Steward, you have a very big dick."

Well, not the plan, but never let it be me who says no. In I go, slowly, softly. She moves a bit from the pain of the insertion. Then relaxes.

Not wanting to kill the poop-shoot, I fucked slowly but with intensity. I wanted to cum fast. And, as I was close from our previous session, it didn't take too long.

I blew off. Damn, it felt good. As good and small as her pussy was, her ass did offer that extra insensitive.

After our encounter, she washed me with the soap, oh so finely. And upon our exit, dried me off with pure excellence.

"Stewart, do you love me?"
"How could I not?"

She pulled me, as she had into the bathroom, out of the bathroom and on to my bed. We made love again.

The evening was upon us and it was not that I was bored with her company but I had expected her to leave on to her appointed rounds of the red light district; money in the bank account and all. To my surprise she, didn't leave and even upon the questioning of the matter declined to remove herself. She did not even wish to go and partake of a romantic candle light dinner. So, we remained—loving as only new lovers can. But, my instantaneous painting, well it certainly was not instantaneously being completed.

Chapter 3

I cannot truly say this brings us up to then—now, where the story begins. But the following two months, give-or-take, seemed to pass by in a blur. A blur of love in the truest sense. For they were days filled with all the anticipation of the next meeting. Filled with all the nights spent making love and sleeping together in each other's arms. The feelings that only new lovers can experience. All the dreams of all the foolish.

She would go off. I would not/could not question where. It's not that I'm a free loving sort of person when it comes to relationships. Nor is it that I didn't care. The matter of the facts being spoken, I'm an intensely possessive and jealous male. This situation, however, had its uniqueness, at least in terms of love or the loves I had previously known.

When we met, I knew what she was. I mean there was no lie going on like had happened to me in the past. And, each time she left I believed I knew where she was going. But when we were together there was more passion and intensity than I had ever known before.

My time would pass when she was not there counting the moments until I saw her again—the moment when she would dance into my field of vision and remove any doubt of what I was doing or why I was doing it.

So, a paragraph for a month or two, the only offering I have to give to the bounds of literature for the time that was spent.

*   *   *

listen wind of the warriors
bleeding into my veins at night
sun stroked vision
of the ultimate emptiness

sun stroke waves in my mind

as your kiss caresses me
form no longer has any value
as your touch reveals to me
what I am—what I have needed
and that there can be nothing more

the praise in parable
hidden beneath the lies
there is a song
where all is promised
but is never given
all is lost
but never found

in the passion
where ideas are forbidden
in the world
which promises only lies
a sacred warrior came to me
gave me everything
how could I question my destiny
how could I walk away

laying bleeding
dying by any other name
the thought, the song, the holy vision
handed to me, so perfectly
Rosie, I love you still

*   *   *

We smoked the powder in her cigarette.

"I need another beer Rosie, to take the edge off this bad shit."
"Edge off?"

She was high. I was high and making the fool's mistake of attempting to get drunk and high. She wasn't going to move. So, I got up, grabbed a brew—grabbed her one and sat back down next to her on the floor.

"Don't you love pong kow, Stewart?"
"I like being high."
"Why haven't you tried it in California?"
"Because in California it is not pure like it is here. Everybody worries if it's heroin at all and not just some messed up garage factory made shit."
"Garage factory?"
"I'll explain it later. In California we do a lot of coke."
"Cocaine?"
"Yes."
"I did that once but I did not get very high."
"Yeah, coke's a subtle high. You have to develop a taste for it, so you know what to observe. It is heaven though."
"Heaven, more than this?"
"Different, very different."

The clouds were forming in my mind as we spoke. It's not difficult to speak on Junk necessarily, yet it seems so fucking useless.

The clouds formed in my mind as they had begun to form in my love or at least the understanding of my love for Rosie. Perhaps it is best that I deviate here just to a bit to explain some of the formation of the clouds that led to doubt or at least the question that was about to be asked.

*   *   *

My friend, my L.A. party bro gives me a call, three days before the above-mentioned powder white session.

"What's going on, etc..."
"I'm in love with a woman!"
"Again... A prostitute, what! If she loved you, man, she wouldn't be a prostitute anymore."

Any-more and be-fore two words that never made sense to me. So, that was that and this was this; be it all as it may.

*   *   *

"Let's make love Stewart."
"I'm fucked up."
"Please... I want to."

She began to undress me. Well not actually undress, she was basically pulling my pants off.

My pup was not so interested, having gained the thorough knowledge of her body over the preceding weeks and with the Junk in flow, well ... She *wanged* on it for a time and with the assistance of a bit of oral aid got me to rise to the occasion.

She pulled off her panties, lifted her skirt, and climbed on top of me. Me, still sitting on the floor, leaning against the couch.

She did most of the action, worked and jerked. I was clouded. I was enthralled. I was distant. I had my mind on other things. She kissed me as she humped.

My mind in its condition, I will not say clouded again, thought back to my telephone conversation three days before—I though back to a time when he and I, my L.A. party friend, had a lady of the evening. The back of a car was the place. We were young. We were drunk. He won the toss of the coin—went first. I got sloppy second. I mounted. I worked. She asked,

"Are you going to cum yet?"
I said, *"Almost."* Though it was a lie.

She began to huff and puff and give me the, *"Oh yeah. Oh yes. Oh baby."* That night, way back when, I pretended to cum—she pretended to cum. A very Zen outcome, I believe. That was a long time ago.

*   *   *

Rosie had, I believed, read my mind. It seemed that she could do that. I don't know how. She really worked it. She came. And, though she usually was one of those chicks to give up after the first cum, kept pumping on. As she did, she said,

"You know Stewart, you are the only one I ever cum with. I never cum with them. Even though some of them try, they can't make me."
"I don't want to talk about it."

She pumped and pumped. I was too fucked up. There was just no way in Hell I was going to cum. I stopped her.
I was lost in the moment, confused. She had cum. Didn't she? Really?

Fucked up, I ask a fucked-up question,

"Do you love me Rosie?"
"I always tell you that I love you Stewart."
"Words are nothing. Do you really love me!"
"Yes, so much. I want to have your baby."
     I laughed to myself.

"Can we go to California soon? I need to get away from here."
"I don't want to talk about that either. There's nothing there for me anymore. I want to go to sleep."

*   *   *

the cancellation of the reward
life it is so limited
absorbed in the nothing
absorbed love—it fades

the cancellation of the intimacy
it had gone to black
wanted and longed for
dreamed of—infatuation fades

it is not clear
life never is
that is life
it is not clear—desire fades

*   *   *

     The escape of sleep, the only remaining medicine.
     In the long breath of silence, I took before I rose and moved in the direction of her bed. I looked out the window. I could see the clouds had all cleared up in the Thailand night time sky. It was so simple, so powder white simple. It was

like the color of forgiveness. It just simply was. I lay down on her bed. I went to sleep.

The morning was bright when I awoke. Bright in terms of a heroin high, a sweet powder white hang over. It was bright, though the drapes they were closed. It was bright through an orange curtain of illumination.

I was awake—Rosie remained enthralled in her dream state next to me. I studied her as she slept. Who was she? An Image? A goddess? A seducer of illusion bringing forth by the devil, giving life and placing it neatly in front of me, precisely upon my lap? Nemesis?

For that matter, who was I? A wayward mystic lost on this pagan shore, kissing the night and finding no further reason to ever leave.

I studied my feelings, bodily as they were. Was I sick? I looked at myself, into myself. Sick? No. What was it I was feeling then?

I thought, I concluded, I understood—it was distance, distance from self. A rather bleak fading feeling. A feeling unable to grab a hold of me, or I on to it.

So, this was the morning after. Power white, as sweet as she was. Powder white, as vague as she is intensifying. Vague, yes. Intensity, yes. Like that of a large city. Not like Bangkok. No, for she is more intense than Bangkok—she is devastating. No, not like Hong Kong, not like L.A., more like London. Yes, London in the winter on a cool and cloudy day. The rain in the distance. Intensity, people, feelings, cars all around. Yet, in the cold, in the clouds there remains a distance—a distance to the intensity. A vague intensity. Vague like the powder white.

I lay there, as is my nature, trying to understand, attempting gain a hold of: life, God, the universe, destiny. I lay there; Rosie began to awake.

*   *   *

in the dawn there is a calm
the calm before the storm
in the morning there seems to be reason
reasons that are lost as the day moves forward

in the rising there is a purpose
dreams/memories of the night before

in all that was
in all that is
in all that will ever come to be
there is a distance
a promise of the distance
a distance, just the same

awake, my sweet Thai flower
awake, open your eyes and embrace the day

*   *   *

"I love you Stewart," were the words that rang as she opened her eyes, turned her body, and touched me as her day begin to take form.

"Why," I wondered. But wonderment, it was all too late for that as she kissed me. Who could wonder as her— Thai lips touched mine.

"Do you feel Okay?" she asked.
"No complaints."
"Make love to me then."

Well, what can I say—to make a long story short, it seemed like an appropriate way to begin the day. I pulled out the sword, it was much more willing the in the evening past. I sent it deep between her Thai legs.

I remained on top. A power trip, as she always liked to play the top role. I pumped up and down, side-to-side, round and round, all of those basic zero missionary position things to do. I realized she came much faster when she was on top. Well, Hell, each girl has her think. I didn't stop thought—wouldn't let myself cum. She tried to roll me over. I didn't let her. I kept going, putting all those ill faded top position tricking in form. Finally, deep into our session. She held me tighter, tighter, tighter. She came.

We lay in bed proceeding our love-making encounter; distant, both of us were distant, I could feel it. Distance is the gift the powder white gives one. The distance of the goddess. Distant, yet so close. She held me. I could feel the agony boiling through the distance, scalding both of our souls. It boiled in her, Rosie, because of her developed pain. It boiled in me, due to the pain that I had developed. Pain is pain all the same.

It was sad as I lay there thinking that both she and I had never chosen our own pain. We both had been dealt similar blows in life. Similar, yet so different. Worlds apart, yet the same. There we were, both of us, in pain. Unnecessary pain, unchosen pain—boiling pain. Yet, the powder, it gave us distance. I then understood why there are so many addicts in this world.

*   *   *

I could feel the encroachment of the alcohol toxin that I should have known better than to drink and combine with the Junk. I felt its poison taking hold. It was one of those oncoming hangover feelings. The kind you get after you are awake for a while. It could have been cured; a little oxygen is all that was needed. But pure oxygen is not what Bangkok is noted for. I would have gotten up, walked for a few miles, in L.A. I would have gone and shot some hoop. But, this was Bangkok, and the air was hot and dirty, while next to me laid all the reason why I could not simply walk away.

Hot, maybe that was the reason. Rosie's apartment, not known for being cool. It was stifling. The air was trapped, no movement, no freedom. An open window bombed by further episodes of hot, humid air. The curtains were closed. Rosie she was Thai, me, I was from L.A. and I never did dig hot. The distance in all its glory began to close in on me.

"I not feeling so good."
"I thought you said that you said you had no complaints."
"I think I've changed my mind."
"You should have barfed Stewart. I told you so."

Beer, now it's not that I don't like it. It's simply that when you pay the price for its consumption it is a very high price to pay.

To dispense with the formalities and get my point across, the remainder of the day I felt none too wonderful. And, post an hour or three of feeling miserable in Rosie's crib, I pulled it together enough to get dressed, pulled up stakes, and made my way down the stairs, and out to the street. Naturally, I had an impossible time getting a taxi. So, I ended up taking an, on the verge of puking, ride home in a *Tuk Tuk* to my *airco'ed* abode. Where the pain was much more tolerable, the distance, much more appreciated, and the bedding far less used.

*   *   *

the kiss of passion
at times it is none too sweet

sweet none too

the reminder of the day
the remainder of the day
when love was lived
when the love was felt
and when the passion fades away

the kiss of passion
placed upon my lips
touched and felt
felt and touched
like holding hands in the park
as the Siam rain begins to fall

Bangkok it is hot
Thailand it is hard
when the moments they are remember
the feeling long and lost
lost and long
but hard to forget

the feelings, they have kissed me
the chances, they have taken hold
like none before
like none could ever do again
promised illusion
paid for with the soul

and the night times they were warm
warm, lost deeply into the goddess's form

she is the illusion
she is my illusion
my dream
my destiny
my demon
She is the truest

and purest form of the night

lose me deeply goddess
lose me in your form
lose me in your illusion
lose me in your lust

and the nights they cried on for remembrance
there was no way to run away
and the longing it kept ringing in my ears
no way to get away
lost forever in the moments of her form
lost forever just the same
I am so lost

* * *

It must have been eight, maybe nine o'clock in the evening when Rosie let herself in and flitted by me, as I was still lying sickly on my bed.

"Hi Stewart."

She oh so graciously made her way directly into my kitchen and oh so artistically pulled the bottle of the vodka out of my freezer.

My mind, it went into regression, studying the memory banks. Two months prior, I thought to myself, it must have been. Can it have been that long ago? Yes, it was. Rosie in all her perfect passion and excellence—I remembered, came into my apartment that night, the next night after; the evening proceeding our first encounter; touching the night that led through to the day next. The night after that day/night, you know.

*　　*　　*

It had indeed been a full-on day, leading to a full-on night. That sweet touch, that first love'n feeling, that first kiss.

The first kiss: when the eyes are closed and you are waiting wondering if, when, it will happen. The perfect kiss. It can never be relived. I remember it, I remember her. I remember Rosie's first kiss so well.

Chapter 4

She had said she must leave. It was the next morning of the first night. She said that she had some business to take care of. The form of which, I most certainly thought that I knew. I sat there, watching her go out the door. I sat there fuming with jealousy, *"Where was my babe going?"* But, I knew that I knew where she was going.

She was gone, left at maybe eleven or twelve in the morning, the morning after. Me, I remained at home that day: pissed off, painting, making expensive international telephone calls to Japan, Hong Kong, Korea, and the States. Calling up other babes on the line and otherwise, proving to myself that I was wanted, really needed by those other than the princesses of the night. I sat at home thinking, "Who needed her?" I was young, American, I could get anything that I wanted and, in fact, planned to do just that, that very evening. Bangkok Discos, look out.

It was maybe eight or nine o'clock that night. I was about to begin getting dressed when through my unlocked door comes Rosie all smiles,

"Hi Stewart."

She looked at me, walked right past me, hit my refrigerator, cracked the freezer open and grabbed the bad dude vodka.

I was almost stunned as I watched her move in for the kill that night. Manners and formalities, I realized never played a part in her life.

That night, it led to a different kiss: an alive kiss, a known kiss. We passed the bottle back and forth, sitting on my couch, Mr. Couch. The bottle was maybe half full to begin with. It was gone in no time at all.

"Do you have another bottle of vodka?"
"Sorry, no."
"Oh well."

She began to kiss me. She put her hand in my pleasure zone and grabbed my dick. She took no prisoners—played no games. She unzipped my pants and lowered her head down over it. Licking, sucking, power driving her thick Thai lips upon my rod of love, moving her hand up and down. She was good. Dick was ready. She kept going on: up and down.

Now, I'm not one to readily cum from a blowjob. Oftentimes, when that's all a bitch is willing to give up, I've got to fantasize that I'm actually fucking to get off, and that takes some time. Rosie's movements were pro though. I was at the point of no return about to spread my love juice upon her tonsils. Just then, she lets loose, raises her head, pulls up her dress and climbed on top of me—slipped the pup right in. No underwear to get in her way. Up and down she moves; faster, faster. Close, I was almost there.

She slides off. I'm in disbelief. Immediately, her heads is down on my cock again, licking sucking. Her Tail red lips stick, again encompassing my dick—up and down. Oh, fuck, I'm into it.

Bam, she stops! Slides her pussy up into the position of passion again. I'm in, she's on. Up and down—up and down, faster, faster, faster. Fuck, I'm there. She stops—like a divine being who knows, who reads my every thought and bodily movement.

In an instant, she's giving me head again. Then the sex. Then the head. Then the sex. The head, the sex, the head, the sex. This went on for a while. Nowhere to turn, no way to stop, Finally, inside of her, I blew it off. The best cum of my life. Even with all these years in the distance, that was the best cum...

"Did you enjoy it, Steward?"

I had no answer.

Without a thought, she guided me up to my feet. Walked me in the direction of the bed. She unzipped her skirt. Took off her blouse. She lay down, extended a hand to me.

"Lets make love again, Stewart."
"Give me a minute."

That minute was short lived. She pulled me towards her. She held me. She kissed me. Dick was back in a big way Rosie and I, we did make love.

Our eyes, they were open; looking at each other, studying each other. They were open; I can see her eyes now. I can look deeply into them, like it was not years ago. She moved, I moved, we made love.

Staring into her eyes, while making love, I realized that our fit, it was perfect; our forms met in harmony. This is not always the case, you know. Sometimes, you must learn to make love to a person. Sometimes, it is no more than a fuck. Sometimes, no matter how hard you try the zero equals only zero and nothing goes nowhere fast.

That was then though, two months before. Two months before this, which is here and what we are discussing.

*   *   *

She grabbed a bottle out of the freezer. She walked in and plopped on the bed.

"Let's get drunk Stewart."
"I'm still sick."

"But this will fix you right up. Then we can do some pong kow."

Now, it's not that I had not spent, previous this, a good percentage of my life at party level one thousand. But, no matter how you slice it, when you are partied down, staring at a bottle of the villain is none too appealing. I avoided the embrace.

"What have you been doing today," I asked.
"Thinking about you."
"Really?"
"Really. I can't wait to get married and go to California with you next week."
"What!"
"That's what you told me last night."
"I don't remember saying that!"
"But, you did. Now you cannot change your mind."

Saying this she leaned over and planted a kiss on me.

"Fuck it, let me have the bottle."

The initial embrace about made me throw up. But, as it came my way the second round, after Rosie had her hit, it went down oh so smooth.

*   *   *

any poison
any passion any
it will do just fine

too many times all alone
when a kiss of the illusion
is all I dreamed of

a kiss of the illusion
a kiss from one of the damned
but as kiss
none the less

and when all the prices have been paid
and when there is no promise for tomorrow
being kiss means more than nothing
any kiss
yes, any kiss will do just fine

*   *   *

Rosie partied hard; there can be no doubt. I guess there is no more perfect way. Well, I can't really say that. The second most perfect way to cover up life lived too long, too hard, and too meaninglessly. The first being the confrontation at the door of the great abyss; the angel of death, you know. She wasn't ready for that and besides the distance developed with the alcohol, the powder white, and the *ganga* made the embrace of life and lust at least tolerable.

*   *   *

The *ganga*—speaking of which, Rosie pulled out a bad pupster and fired it up. Now, personally, *ganga,* (marijuana), is not particularly my scene. It makes me too spaced out and I don't really like the feeling it produces. I don't really like that feeling, that is not saying that I don't do it periodically.

We hit it hard, *the ganga*. We hit it hard, the vodka; killing the first round, three quarter full bottle and taking a big notch out of another one I had appropriately stashed. We hit them both hard. My head had entered into the mode of spin. We hit them both hard before Rosie even pulled out

The Dog, the powered white. I was smacked a bit too hard though, I said, *"No thank you."* She looked at the vile, it slipped from her hand, and she passed out. I was soon to follow, but not before the thought came to mind of how our love was fading, fading fast into the zone of the chemical abyss. Too fast, two months fast. We spent most of our time, partied down.

Fading into not making love all the time, even a vague disinterest in the making of love to her at all. Vague, like the *pong kow* makes life feel. Vague, yes. Very-very vague.

*   *   *

The powder had already begun to lead me to the doorway of the demon. I'm the fool who didn't see the approach of no way out. Rosie knew the door well for she had knocked at it many a time.

It was a month before, maybe three weeks, maybe five. Exact time fades into the lost realms of lost memories.

The door was being opened for me, an uncloseable door. Once you are touched, you may never be untouched again. Yes, the door was opening and I did not see that it was to close behind me, close behind me and lock me in.

I believe in signs. All seems to be revealed before action is ever taken—before the life experience is ever lived. That is self-evident. It was soon to be my sign. I did not see it.

*   *   *

Rosie wanted to pick up some of the *pong kow*. It was the first and the only time I had ever accompanied her to the doorway of the demon.

There is this street in Bangkok. For literary sake and to save the souls of the masses it is best that I don't name it, do not describe it too well. But, it is a street where the *pong kow* dealers abound and sell their commodity.

It's not far from a hotel, a major chain hotel, in which I have inhabited long ago in the past. It's not far from the now booming tourist shopping trade, a district tourist road. No, it's not far.

Falong, (foreigners), may be seen in the vicinity all the time. In the vicinity, but not of the vicinity. In the vicinity, in their ignorance. In the vicinity, but not in the state of mind of the vicinity. In the vicinity, in search of gifts. But, not the gifts, not the kind that powder white brings. Fuck tourists, they are losers anyway...

Her, Rosie's usual connection had to do a journey up North. The golden triangle called his name. North of Chiang Rai. North, where the *pong kow* flourished in its maiden form. Fields of flowers staring softly at the Thailand sky. Poppies blowing gently in the wind, seeking only the blind stare of the ancient Asian moon.

It is a beautiful land up there. I have been there many a time. Beautiful, where people carry rifles and machine guns. Beautiful, where you must pay the police their corruption toll just for driving down the road—or, you never know where you will be taken, and you may never be seen again.

Yes, he was out of town: Rosie had her desires— Rosie had her needs. We, we were in love.

"Will you go with me Stewart?"
"Sure, why not."

*   *   *

As the embrace draws near the night time close
in the moments when nothing but love can be seen
yes, it always the answer
yes, it is surrender

yes, is what is said
even if it should not be said

*   *   *

Perhaps it was karma. Perhaps it was destiny. Perhaps I had been living on borrowed time for too long. But, a Bangkok friend of mine had lent me his car for the day. The motion in progress, we went outside and were hit with the killer heat. I opened the door for Rosie as she climbed into the metallic silver boxy Japanese made automobile. She got in. I walked to the right side and I got in. I started the car. Turned on the air conditioning and we drove off.

I knew of the street we were headed to. I had heard its tales before. I didn't like the idea. But I went anyway.

Bangkok is a ridiculously designed city. One-way streets that go on for miles. Traffic jams that continue for hours. We went down and around. I turned right and finally there they all were on the corner.

I pulled up. Everyone knew why I, a *falong* and she, a Thai, had pulled up. Everyone but the tourists. I didn't see any, anyway.

I pulled up and all the demons disciples ran to the car. I didn't like the feeling—the obvious nature of what was going down. Eight or ten Thai men came up to the window that Rosie's head peered out of. Several more stood in front, looking in. It made me fucking paranoid.

"That was easy," I thought, as we drove away. It only took a second, a moment of negotiation; bought and sold in a time bound only to reality by these words of written posterity.

I pulled away from the curb and out onto the street in question. Up ahead at the end of the block, automobiles in heat. The bout of the metal on wheels; gridlock, maybe a quarter of a mile in length. The fucking Bangkok traffic jams, they are just kill. We were going nowhere fast.

I wanted to get off that street. Man, I was steaming with that feeling of knowing you've done something wrong and having to stand there and look at it. I wanted distance, space, to be lost from the scene of the crime. Traffic and Bangkok did not choose to cooperate though. Paranoia set in deep.

Rosie continued to assure me that there was nothing to worry about; this was Thailand, not California. People purchased *pong kow* there all the time. The police knew all about it. My paranoia, aided undoubtedly by the traffic jam, continued to grow incessantly.

We finally turned right onto a main, get out of Dodge fast, thoroughfare. I turned right, but there he was, a policeman. Standing in back of a Bangkok police car. He stepped off the curb, pointed his Thai finger at the ground. I was to pull over.

There were no questions asked, words were only spoken in Thai. He opened my door, grabbed my arm, and pulled me out. I thought to forcibly escape his grip; hit the cop hard. Maybe break his knee and run. But run to where? This was a main street in Bangkok. It was not like that one time, once a long time ago; out there in the Thai distance, a previous and former Thai love riding shotgun.

*   *   *

Her and I, that former Thai love, Manita, we proceeded our way through the Golden Triangle night. *En route,* much later than we had expected, back to Chiang Mai. A policeman, corrupt as all of those *mutha' fuckers* are, at one of those set up in the night road side stops—out there in the far side of midnight. He stopped us; first he wanted money. I didn't speak much Thai back then or I would have argued. I was pissed, but I gave him some Thai Bhat. Then he wanted her, my babe, my love; the person I actually thought to bring back to L.A. with me. He said, *"She must be a bad girl, being with a falong."* He and the other policeman had us get out, wanted to do her in the back seat of their official Thai government ride.

They took me out of the car too, that was their mistake. I walked up close to one, stared at him right in the eyes. This made the other one come closer. They, close and together; I took both of those *mutha' fuckers* out. A Knife Hand to the throat of the one on my side, a pivot, a two-handed grab—one to the front, one to the rear. A snap of the other dude's neck. They were down, dead. Fuck 'em. There was no way in the fucking world that they were going to have my lady just because they had the badge and the power. They shouldn't have messed with me. They were out-a-there. We were out-a-there—deep in the Thailand night.

I was scared then too. In Chiang Mai the next morning, I got a flight to Bangkok, then to Hong Kong. The babe well, it never worked out. The joke was on me... Turned out she was a way far Thai slut of a looking for any *falong* that she could find. Didn't learn that until forty or fifty thousand dollars later though. But that night, her honor, it stayed intact.

*   *   *

And Rosie, what about Rosie? I couldn't jam them up and leave her. I tell you, I was seriously pulsating.

Rosie's door was open by an additional cop on the beat. She was speaking Thai too fast for me to really understand. She was offering them money: Thai money, U.S. money. She handed them her entire purse. The *pong kow* was in the purse. I thought what a stupid move.

My heart pounded, intensely pounded. If I hadn't been sweating from the heat already, I would have begun to.

Up in front of the police car was a small Thai style police pick-up truck. It almost looked military: green, khaki. It had a khaki canvas enclosure over the back of it. I was worried. Big time worried.

The policeman took my arm, led me to the back of the truck. Opened the canvas back, there were three Thai policemen inside. He told me to get in. I looked; Rosie was being pulled by her arm, arguing all the way. She was told to get in.

"I am American!"

I kept saying it—yelling it in English. I too was scared. I could not bring the words forward in Thai.

American, big deal. How many Americans are there in Thai prisons for similarly chasing the powder white goddess?

We were in the back of the truck, not hand cuffed, just sitting surrounded by the three Thai cops. I guess they figured with the three policemen there we were not going to do much.

Me, I thought of taking them all out, there and then. It wouldn't have been so hard to do, for they closed the canvas rear opening and there was almost no light. I could have hit 'em hard—hit 'em deadly.

Rosie kept arguing and offering them money. I kept asking her what are they doing, where are they taking us. She didn't answer.

The dark closed in on me, as I felt life was about to do.

We hadn't driven far, maybe ten minutes away or so. The truck stopped. I could hear the two front doors open and another car pull up and stop behind us. Our back, rear canvas flap was opened. The light hurt my eyes. One of the inside policemen grabbed my arm, another grabbed Rosie's and they led us out, while holding on to their rifles.

His grip was tight. I remember it well. Tight, but I could feel that he was not strong. Tight like the kind of grip that takes all of one's strength to give. He'd be no match for me.

It was a side street, a street that I did not know. There were houses, rather large houses. One was orange. Yes, I remember one was orange over to my right. Over on the other side there were others, I do not remember them well.

To my left, in front of me was this rather office building looking type structure: four stories, white; dirty white like all Thailand white is. The building had windows, windows but no signs.

Rosie kept yelling. I could see tears form in her eyes; rough eyes, hardened eyes, the kind that never cry.

I wanted to know where we were. Rosie did not answer.

They led us inside. The building was dirty, like Thailand is dirty. The walls were wood, dark wood, not the color of the wood you usually see in Thailand. There was a desk. A uniformed lady sat at the desk. The desk was wood, dark wood. They led us to the stairs. The stairs were wood, dark wood. They were wide. They led us up to the second floor, into an office, a large office. The policeman still held my arm. He sat me down. They continued to take Rosie through another door. A dark wood door, leading into another office.

"Where are they taking you?"

No answer.

They sat me down. The policeman let go of my arm. He sat down next to me in a similar dark wood chair, holding onto his rifle that he had not let go of. Another officer sat down across the dirty white room from us. He sat in a chair similar to ours. He too held his rifle.

I thought of Rosie. I could hear her voice, yelling.

I counted the numbers. Two in the room with me, both with guns. I being the long trained martial artist that I was could take them out no problem; fast and easy. There were at least three with Rosie; armed. I could take them down, as well. I could, if I could get to them before they knew I was coming and got to their guns. But, I didn't know where they were or how they were stationed. I knew if I went for the fight, I would have to go for the kill or there would never be a way out—no way out of Thailand. My adrenaline was surging, I was shaking from its force. I was ready. I couldn't leave Rosie. I was ready to kill. I would die before going to a Thai prison. Then I heard Rosie's voice yelling no more.

I sat there for a time: ten, fifteen minutes, I don't know. I thought of if I attacked, how could I explain the car. Could they find me through it—through my friend? I wondered if I could get out of the country in time?

I was wondering why weren't the policemen speaking to me. They were silent and except for one smoking, there was no other sound in the room.

I wonder why this office had only chairs: four on one side, three on the other, and nothing else placed upon its hard wood floors.

Mostly, I thought of Rosie. Where had they taken her, and what were they doing to her? I was burning.

The man who had pointed his Thai finger at me to pull my friend's Japanese made car over, walked through the door. Out through the door to the inner office where they had taken Rosie. He said to me in English.

"You like *pong kow?*"

I said nothing.

"What you name American man?"

I said nothing.

"What you name!" he yelled.
"Stewart, Stewart Shangrila."
"How much money you have America man?"
"Where's my friend?"
"You worry about you! How much money you have?"
"With me, I don't know. Let me look."

The truth being told I knew just about exactly how much I had. In Asia, I used to have this, now recognized, bad habit of carrying five or six hundred dollars on me in U.S. currency at all times. I figured if I ever needed it, I would have it. Well, I needed it.

I pulled my Thai money out and began counting it. He grabbed it.

"This is nothing, are you a poor boy? I hope you not poor boy. I hope you have America money! Do you have America money?"

Now this game was getting tight and I did not feel like playing it a bit. There's no doubt in any one's mind of the corruption in the Thailand government. This was pushing it though and pushing me. I tried to play it off but saw no way out. My heart pounded. I thought of the freedom of my beach apartment in L.A. I thought how could I have been so fucking stupid. I thought of Rosie.

Fear, there are no words that ever can describe it. My chest pounded with it. I sweated it. Sweated it over the already hot Thai sweat that lay upon my skin. I breathed it. I could hardly breath.

"Where's my friend?"
"You friend dirty girl! You like dirty girl, America man?"

He obviously knew of her profession of the night. I was worried.

"Where is she?"
"How much U.S. money you have, falong?"

I looked through my wallet casually. As cautiously as possible, that is, with the three policemen; one on each side, the other in front of me looking on. I tried to pull the cash out exposing as little as possible.

"One hundred dollars. Oh good, America man."

He grabbed my wallet.

"You lie, America Man!"

He began to tear it apart—looking in all the stash compartments and found all the other hundred-dollar bills I had. I saw him counting the money. He looked at me and smiled. Then he went for my credit cards.

"Platinum American Express, good card. Diners Club, MasterCard, Visa. You big man, yes?"
"No."

He said something to the other Thai cops; they looked at me and went into the other office.

"You lucky man, America man. You big man. You go now."

He threw my now empty wallet at me.

"Where's my friend?"

"You America man. She Thai girl. You go. You very lucky man."

"What about my car?"

"Thai car, you America man. You go now!"

It was obvious he was getting pissed, though that certainly didn't bother me—that pussy of a corrupt cop. I would like to meet him out on the street.

I knew that there was nothing that my screaming back at him would prove. It would only get me in deeper shit. Out the door I went.

I walked down the stairs and the woman at the desk smiled and said goodbye to me in Thai. I said nothing.

Outside, it did feel good. Good, like you can't fucking believe. Like a freedom you have never know, until you lose it. A freedom that you have never really experienced. Bliss in the wind.

I was confused. I didn't know what to do. I mean I couldn't even call a cop.

I walked down the street towards a more heavily trafficked street I saw in the near distance. I wanted to be seen. Not that it would help any. Not with the fear the Thai people had of Thai police. But I didn't want to be isolated.

I walked, my breath pounded with my heart. I was so angry I couldn't believe it.

I got to the main street and stood there staring back at the building. I thought to go to the American Embassy. But little help they would give to me, a wayward stranger popped on a *pong kow* bust. I stood there. I looked for a sign.

My mind went to Rosie, it scorched with jealousy. Jealousy that I had kept hidden deep, locked away, since we had been together. It burned, it hurt, it made me want to scream or to cry. It was like maybe thirty minutes later, thirty minutes spent in despair. I was still staring at the building, still waiting for a sign. I saw Rosie exit. It was like a divine vision.

"Rosie!"

She walked towards me, I towards her. As we approached I noticed a smile on her face.
"We sure got out of that one," she said.
"Did they do anything to you?"
"Do what?"

Rosie laughed.
I wish I could have taken it as easy as her. We walked back up to the main street. She signalled a Taxi. It stopped. We got in.

"They took my money, Rosie, how are we going to pay for this?"
"Don't worry, I want to stop at my friend's apartment."

She didn't say anything as the taxi drove through the Bangkok streets. I didn't say anything. Not for the rest of the ride. My heart pounded, from the fear, from the jealousy, from being ripped off. But, I knew what we did was illegal and it was my own fault.

We arrived at her friend's apartment building. A friend that I had not known of before. She told the driver in Thai to wait. She told me in English to wait. Fifteen, twenty minutes later she re-arrived new purse in hand. She had emerged from the office building purse-less.

We drove on. Out of her new bag she pulls a vile, a container. She wanted me to look at what her friend had given her; *pong kow.* I wished, to myself that we would have just gone there before.

The taxi pulled up in front of my apartment building.

"Have to go to work Stewart. Bye bye."

"Bye bye," that was it. She was gone. I stood there watching the taxi drive off down the dirty Bangkok street. Drive her off to the night. Drive her off to the arms of another. Her off and me alone. Alone, like I had come to Thailand. Alone, like I had forever been. Alone.

What the fuck was going on? I had no idea. I wanted to speak of our experiences. I thought I knew what happened to her. I knew what had happened to me but she let me out. She drove off, *"Bye bye."* Bye bye, off into her world. She cured her pain, by inflicting more pain. Me, I had no cure.

Into my crib. I telephoned America that night, told them to tell them, the credit card companies, that my cards had been stolen. Send new ones my direction. America sounded good, sounded simple. But, I knew I had no simplicity there either.

I telephoned the friend whose car I had borrowed, he was mega pissed. He told me I would have to be the one to pay the bribe to get the car back and he would never let me use it again.

That day had turned out to be expensive...

What is sex to a hooker, I tried to tell myself. I tried to tell myself that as I lay in bed shaking from fear, shaking from anger, shaking from adrenaline. Maybe had there been someone else around, I could have been stronger, would have been stronger. But I was alone, really alone. I felt like I did when I was a young child.

But that was before all this. A month or so before. That month that I tried to sum up in a paragraph or so back then. Before, I had touched the realm of the goddess and came knocking at the door of the demon—open in part and in fact by Rosie, my lady of the evening love.

Yes, that was all before. The before that I said I would not deviate to. I will try not to let it happen again.

Chapter 5

Morning falls hard sometimes in its wisdom.

Oh, just for your information, I'm back to the storyline here… You know, where Rosie came over and we dank some vodka.

So anyway, to reiterate, morning falls hard sometimes in its wisdom. I never was one who enjoyed getting out of bed, driven by an alarm clock. Me, I prefer to lie there; ponder life, existence, and reality for a time. Sometimes it's too much of a time.

I awoke, Rosie was gone. Somehow it all seemed so appropriate, so necessary, and so perfect. But then, life always is; perfect you know—divinely perfect.

Sometimes we do not see the perfection, however. The perfection of the moment. How it, may all lead us somewhere, somewhere else. Somewhere which may, as somewhere always is, nowhere.

*　　*　　*

Rosie was not there that A.M. She had left, while I drunkenly slept.

I was sick, mega sick—major hangover. It slapped me fast, hard. Hard, the joke was my dick was hard. A piss hard-on, and in this condition. The joke, as it always seems to be, was on me.

I had to pull myself from bed and hit the head. I walked. I stumbled. I looked around. My apartment was a mess. It always seems my apartment is a mess.

There I was in Thailand. Thailand, land of the maids. I should have had a maid.

There never seems to be enough time to take care of all the foolish business of the clean it up world and still be creative. It always all seems like such a fucking waste of time; the mundane, you know. I don't know, but I already talked about this didn't I. Anyway, enough of my going off on a tangent and back to the so-called literature.

*   *   *

there is a kiss in the morning
the morning as late as it may be
known/felt
it can never be forgotten
lost/gone
but it will forever be remembered

kiss me again
don't make me wake up alone

*   *   *

I, as I stood there hanging one, decided it would no doubt make me feel a whole lot better if I were to take a shower. So, a shower seemed the course of action. I turned it on, waited for it to reach an appropriate temperature of warmth and climbed in. As I did, as the water hit me, as the wetness embraced me, my mind it went numb. The starry sparkles came to my eyes, my head spun. It all became dark. I fell down. I grabbed the shower curtain. It came down with me. It was white—white in Thailand. Not Thailand dirty white. My tub was white, porcelain white.

It took me a few seconds as I lay there attempting to grasp onto what was happening to me—lay there holding onto the side of the tub like a drunken suicidal slime. I lay there, for a few seconds that felt like hours, realizing that the water was way too hot. Hot, as it hit me. Hot, as my head spun on. Hot, I wanted it to be cooler, but I could nothing.

I fought to hold onto consciousness. I knew I must make my mind focus on a thought. A thought, any thought.

Any thought that would hold me close enough to reality to keep me from passing out. The only thought that came to mind, was the thought of Rosie.

Rosie, her essence was in my field of subconscious vision.

Rosie, her thought perpetuated my mind. It was like a vision, a hazy vision. Like a goddess on an old black and white television set where the picture, the focus was none too clear. Rosie in all her dark, feminine, and fine glory stood there. It was as if she tried to hold me, as if I tried to reach her. Tried but was unable to.

As I grasped at her, it was like her vision became a field of red. Deep red—blood red. My mind raced to a time when I was maybe seven years old and first heard someone speaking of their first-hand experience with the drug LSD. I had gone to work with my mother. I had gone to spend the day. A day in youth when time was not so important, not so little of it left. I was assigned, my job of the day was to sit on a chair and watch the back the door. Watch it so no one could make away with the female garments that waited to be shipped to stores around L.A. As I performed my duties, two young Latin men spoke. One described his experience with the hallucinogenic and told the tale of how each time it was ingested just before he came on, he would have a flash of red, bright red, blood red. He claimed it to be the sign of the devil—that drugs were a devil's high. I wondered why if they were demonic, he continued to use them.

Perhaps it was his words etched into my young mind. Perhaps it is truth—I do not really know. But, when it was my turn to take control of the altered realm, take the bull by the horns, I too had the experience of the flash of red, deep red, blood red.

It was that color which permeated my vision as I sat, hanging onto the side of my bathtub.

Rosie had turned into a demon, a Thai demon with a spear that stabbed into my heart. Red, deep red, blood red flowed from my body, from my stabbed heart. It surrounded me. It covered me. It blanketed everything that I saw. It spurted on me, as the spear was removed from my body with my heart intact upon its point.

That is the last thing I remember. My spinning had stopped, for I had stopped.

I don't know exactly how long I lay there in that position, but I was finally awakened by the feeling of the cold water from the shower covering my body.

Perhaps it was good that my apartment had a small water heater. I however, always hated the fact that it would run out of warm water before I had completed my traditionally long showers. But perhaps it served its purpose. All things being perfect, you know.

As my mind came back to consciousness, it was almost with a jump. For my body lay there shivering as the cold water poured over me. Shivering cold, in maximum hot Thailand. I tried to get up; it was not easy.

I reached for and turned off the shower. I pulled myself up to a seated position. My head still spinning, I tried once again to grab a hold on reality.

My body shivered. I wished for the warmth of the hot Thai climate I knew was blistering outside. But I couldn't make it, all I could was grabbed a towel wrapped it around me as I sat there trying to figure out what had happened.

It took me some time but I pulled myself up, checked my look in the mirror to confirm that my heart had not actually been removed on the end of a spear. I studied myself, confirming no external damage had been done to my form. I headed back to bed, still wet. Seeking the comfort and warmth of the angelic pillows and covers.

I lay there in bed with my head still spinning, hurting from a headache. My stomach feeling on the verge of puking from the two consecutive nights of drink. I once again swore to myself, the hangover promise of, *"Never again."*

*   *   *

wind spills its wisdom
it never claims to take form
rain moves its passion
silent, yes so silent

the rain in the evening calls me
the wind in the day leads me
and their essence overtakes me
promising me everything
everything in the dawn

the night in its absences
promises magic
and tomorrow the magic leads to
never-never land
it takes me away

and all the ancients
in all their perfect manifestations
and all the sinners
in all their foolish games
and all the dreamers
that laugh until they cry
never have they touched the deepest realms
where no light has ever been seen

so you can sing to me all your praises
you can tell me all your lies
you can laugh at me/call me a fool
but essence is as essence does
so cry
when you know the secret of pain
so lie
and you can hear the secret of truth

so touch
and you feel the secret of longing
so die
and you will feel the secret of life.

*   *   *

It must have been two days before I really felt AOK. AOK enough to hit the streets and the outside again. Yes, it must have been two days before I pulled it together enough to head out and down to this little Bangkok restaurant that I like to frequent.

It's generally said that the hang over shift lasts only a day. Somehow that has just not been the case with me. As I've aged and the years have come on, it's more like: two, three, four, five days plus before I feel fully straight again once the villain alcohol and or other substance has taken hold.

Two days, and Rosie had not phoned, had not come over. Now this was not, in fact, all that unusual but call me a romantic, I felt after all we had gone through she would have at least had the decency to chill on by or ring me up on the tele. But I mean hey, fuck her, if she wants to play that way.

I went out the door and on to the Bangkok streets – the back streets. It was hot; dirty hot. I wondered how I could have ever desired to be embraced by this heat as I lay there shivering in the depths of a freezing cold shower two days before.

I was out though, and out felt good. I gave myself a little, *"Owh"* as I proceed to get a taxi without too much difficulty and headed on to the restaurant in mind with the intention of placing a bit of protein in my system. I swore to myself that I would never undergo another session with the booze, the ganga, or the powder white.

I arrive; I was welcomed, as always, with hands in traditional prayer position and Thai style hello, *"Surwahdee."*

The food went down good. It felt right to eat out, outside again. I finished the food, *java-ed* myself down with a cup of that bad Thai brew; stiff coffee that is. I was alive. Alive, all dressed up and no place to go.

As I pounded down the last drops of the coffee, I realized that I didn't want to just go home. So, I walked out of the air-conditioned cafe and onto the sizzling hot street.

I thought to visit Rosie; first thought best thought and all. But no, I was just not ready for that. It would be like I was running to her, you know. And though it was difficult for me to take my mind off of her—after all I was a bit in love, a bit pissed, and a bit of a few things in between. But, she had not contacted me—and I mean hey, if they don't want to know then forget 'em. It's the babe's job to come a-run'n.

As I paced my way down the street I had this feeling come over me of the uselessness of life. It was a mental thing, a physical sensation too. I feel it in my mouth, in my heart, my brain reverberated it. Like what the fuck is the point to Rosie, to being in Thailand, to life itself.

The feeling pulsated in me, but with my relatively on the return to a healthy body in tow, I decide to go and visit my sweet French friend who had initially and, in fact, introduced me to Rosie.

Chapter 6

Patricia, born and raised in Bangkok. French in blood line, but her features, her actions Thai—people chameleons as they are...

Have you ever notice that? How people once they are placed in a culture, a country, different from their indigenous race and are allowed to live, grow from an early age form the features, the tongue, and the actions of the locals.

Anyway, Patricia, in fact, once married to a Thai rock star but that was years ago. She was young then—fifteen and pregnant. She has a boy. A boy and a passion. The boy mostly raised by her parents. Her passion, the Junk.

Maybe I could have loved her if I would ever have given myself a chance. Well sure, I loved her. But not in that way, you know. We go back a bit, her and I. A year, two, three, or four. Before, before that, before the powder white session(s) began.

"I haven't seen you in two months, Stewart. Where the fuck have you been. I thought maybe you went back to the States."

Nice greeting, I thought, as she came to answer the door.

Showing up unannounced, I know it's not so polite but this was Bangkok where formality goes out the window and besides, what are friends for?

"I would never leave without telling you goodbye." I said in my most passionate voice.
"Besides, my telephone hasn't been ringing off the hook from calls from you either."
"Oh, you know me Stewart, I have been busy."

Busy, yeah, I knew. It does take a lot of time for one to chase their passion.

Chasing passion... I have known the feeling well.

*   *   *

Do you ever stop and review the conversations that go on between people? Sometimes when I'm in them or other times upon later reflection, they all seem to amount to nothing—not a thing at all.

Patricia and I spoke, as people speak. About nothing—nothing in general. Comparison of notes on the abstract. Abstraction; words to say, when words no longer have any meaning.

"Oh, you've tried the pong kow! You love it, don't you? I knew you would. What! Rosie turned you on to it. You're still hanging out with her?"

The vague jealousy rose. Rose of Rosie. Yes, it must be true; she could have loved me, as well. Our new subject of conversation, our new reason to speak. And the nothing was interrupted by a moment of another passion; jealousy.

The subject as per my command faded into the more relevant discussion of the substance. She suggested,

"You want to do some, Stewart?"

Now, the relevance of my newfound two-day sobriety seemed to fade by the wayside, aided in no small part by the promise of something, as opposed to nothing. I don't know, sometimes just the meaninglessness of life overtakes you: when no answers are given and there is no one to hold you, telling you the lie, that it all means something, that it will all be all right. And as long known the promise of illusion was much more alluring than another day on the so-called wagon.

"Let's do it."

*   *   *

Patricia lived in this more than beautiful house in, I guess, what would be considered the semi-suburbs of Bangkok. Well, it was at least off the beaten path of the cars, the pollution, and the people. The main house was large. The property was large. Patricia however, lived in the guesthouse in the back. The guesthouse in the back. Giving her the distance needed for the distance. The pursuit of her passion.

We left the main house, passed one of the family maids, *"Surwahdee."*

We walked the planks that went across the densely grassed lawn that lead from one structure to the next. The planks to protect from the infamous Thai night time reptiles, i.e. snakes that roam freely in the semi coolness, semi dampness of the Thai night-time. She opened the door; we entered her guesthouse abode. A single room with a double bed. A double bed and a private bathroom. All that and a patio too—just outside, which faced into the realms of nowhere. The place Junk best describes. The place life leads to and what life is all about.

She reached under the clean white, not Thai white bedspread, in between the mattress and the box springs out was a produced a key. A key that went to unlock a white drawer; clean white. Out of which she pulled a vile with the powder white: clean white, pure white, Thai powder white.

She led me to her patio. The heat was still on. I sat down upon one of the two chairs that resided in said location.

"How do you want to do this Stewart?"
"You don't smoke it?"

"No, not really. Let me show you a new way, something you obviously have not tried before with little miss lady of the evening."

Patricia's jealousy was popping through again.

"I'll be right back."

She entered the guesthouse. I was alone, worried; worried of the needle that was about to pierce my arm. Concerned of how to nicely say, *"Let's just smoke it the way I did before."* Say it to my jealous friend.

Patricia re-emerged with nothing evident, nothing to show for her journey inwards. I felt almost a bit relieved.

"How's this for fun?"

She produced a straw hidden in her hand.

"If you really want a kick, this is the way to do it."

A straw and a drug, something right up my alley. My anxiety vanished. My wonderment began. Up the nose, all-right.

Patricia dumped a bit of the substance on the table, the small patio table that lay between us. The table was white, Thai dirty white. She dumped it out. Did not even chop it up, razor blade style, like we do with the coke in L.A. She just dumped some out, moved it around with the small straw; didn't even draw up lines just plopped down her face and zipped up a nose load.

"No art in formation here," I thought. The forming of the perfect line being quite the objective in my days of the cocaine usage. *"No art here. And, this table is dirty. I'm going to get a bunch of Thai dirt up my nose."* I didn't like it, did not like it at all.

Patricia leaned back, sniffed it in and up a few more times, passed the straw my direction.

Well, what's a guy like me supposed to do? I went down; bap, I hit me a hard one.

"Fuck, this definitely does have a numbing kick."

As I immediately merge into the *veg-zone* of *never-never land*. Patricia began to laugh.

Now, just let me put things this way, in the *pong kow* up the nose-snorting department—*caine* you can do up nice and neat. And sure, you may destroy your nose in the long run but no pain no gain, right? I mean you can hit the line, those that are so artfully drawn up with the razor blade, and feel it caressing your nostril as it goes up and in—heaven in the making, awaiting the come on. Then there's *crank,* that bad truck driver of a drug that I have indulged in once or thirty times. You do not even think of letting it go straight up your nose or it will burn the hell out if it; being the dirty East L.A. drug factory produced intoxicant that it is. You have to put that straw way up in that bad nostril or it is the burning fire of suicide destruction on the old nose. I mean you pump it in and you are ON. But if you do just a hint too much you may as well kiss the world goodbye *mutha' fucker* because it is going straight for the heart and you are going to die *muy pronto*. Heroin though, it is not that way. It's like when you snort it; this numbing bliss that quickly over takes you and not a damn thing matters at all.

It took some time, maybe a whole three minutes or so, until I was *Gonesville Daddy-O*—into the total numb that the Junk brings on. It was time for another try.

Patricia, had already bent over and gone down I think two more times before I had redeveloped the courage to stroke my nostril again. The straw at my nose, I leaned over, face to the table and up it went. Though I did still feel a bit of a numbing sensation, it was far less than the last time around and the coming on was far more mellow, if you catch my meaning. As we continued, I began to once again no longer feel anything. The perfect feeling.

Maybe forty-five minutes or so into our session, the Thai rain begins to come down. Now in Thailand, it doesn't just rain—I mean sure there is water and all, but in Thailand it really rains. It rains crocodile tears. Hard and fast with its movement cutting like a knife; they are sharp as a dagger. I sat there looking at all of Gods majesty. I let it knife me, stab me in the heart, kill me oh so slowly. It was perfect. I wanted to die, for nothing else in life promised anything more than the perfection of death.

"Let's go inside Stewart, I'm getting wet."

The rain had begun to blow onto us as we three sat: Patricia, the *pong kow,* and I…

"I like it here. I don't want to move."
"You're high, Stewart."
"No doubt."

Patricia spooned the remaining powder white, which was still on the table, back into the vile. She blew the rest into the wasteland with a breath that came from the gods. She got up and pulled me along behind her.

I don't really remember the movement but looking around I noticed we had entered her room. I was looking up, looking up from lying on her bed: the white one, with the white bedspread. I was looking up, I was laughing. Patricia was sitting next to me, ploughing her way through some more Junk that she had now laid out on her nightstand.

I pulled myself up to join her at her vice. I was swaying. I was out of it big time. Out of it and I liked it.

As I pulled myself up and leaned over to give my nose its way, I kind of fell into Patricia. I leaned on her shoulder—laughing, we were both laughing.

My nose finally found its way to the powder, up and in it went. I felt the sensation, knew I had returned to old habits, old tricks. But I was high, very high, and definitely higher than the last time around—the last time with Rosie. Maybe it was due to the snorting. Maybe it was due to the amount of consumption. Maybe, I did not know, I did not care.

"Fuck that shit," I slurred, more or less to myself.
"What?" Asked Patricia, slurring as well.
"Nothing."

She was getting up—up to hit the head. Obviously she had to go and puke. Me, I fell back on her bed. Fell back, as she, my support exited. It was Okay, I thought, AOK. Junk and alone, my mind sent itself into reflection, regression. I checked, I looked hard, very hard but nothing mattered at all.

Patricia came back in and sat next to me,

"Why are you still friends with that street walker?"
"Why are you," I asked.

No answer. I felt the thoughts; the jealousy being put to play once again. How could she think of such things at a time like this? I wondered how she could kept her thoughts so concise when the nectar of the gods, the soma, ran through our bodies—was absorbing into our blood, caressing our brain—as the cosmic suction, as the divine seduction took control of our souls and led us on a path few mortals have ever travelled.

"Do you want a girlfriend Stewart?"
"Huh?"

"I want to be your girlfriend. Make love to me."

With this, she began to take off her top. As she did, she kind of fell over and was lying down next to me. I looked through my peripheral vision. I saw her exposed stomach, thirty or forty pounds overweight. I saw her struggling to unfasten her bra. Finally, it popped open, exposing her breast. Large white breasts, something I had not seen for awhile. White and fluffy, just not my *thAng*.

My peripheral vision faded, I faded, faded to the realm where no man of this world can touch in waking state. I went to sleep.

*   *   *

I groggily awoke. It took me a few minutes to figure out where I was and how I had gotten there, but the thoughts were put in their order quickly enough. I looked over to my right and there was Patricia laying as she had the night before—in a fading memory of her proposal, with her legs hanging over the side of the bed and her breasts exposed.

I was stiff. Not in the sexual sense, but my body having slept sideways across the bed all night obviously jammed close to hers felt not too right. I tried to twist and turn a bit, to loosen up but I was trapped in the cage that God had placed me in; my own skin.

I could not really tell if it was light outside, for Patricia had these wooden, painted white of course, shutters on the interior of her windows and they were closed. The light from the previous evening was still on which clouded by ascertaining, as well. I, however, heard the chirping of birds outside. So yes, it must be morning.

As my senses began to gradually return, I studied the outline of the form that lay next to me, lost deeply in the realities of drug-induced sleep. Mostly, I saw her white breasts. Perhaps that is where my mind chose to most directly focus. They were large and had a flabby quality to them; obviously due to the birth of her child, her son, at such a young age. They had more than a few stretch marks outlining and depicting their form and formation. Her skin, milky white, not the caramel color of many a French person. But white, very white. I was rising to attention, if you catch my meaning.

I rolled over a bit, and due to the invitation of the previous night, decided to now take her up on her offer. My tongue found its way upon her nipples. They tasted as if she had not taken a bath for a day or two. Well, she was French. None-the-less, I went at them for a time and had just made contact with the bush down below; having ran my hand up the white linen skirt that she wore and up and over her underwear. Then she began to cough.

She jumped up, looked around.

"Stewart," she said with a smile.

She then lunged up and ran for the bathroom. I could hear her puking. I'm sorry, but the mood it was broken.

She walked out of the bathroom, her top still open, and her breasts still exposes. Her bra hung there over her plump stomach, like a fallen wreath on a windy forgotten grave.

Her entrance, all smiles with delusions of impending lust in her eyes. She planted herself next to me and tried to lay a slob. I veered to the right, feinting her attack, as nicely as I could.

"Do you feel all right Patricia?"
"Yes, I feel fine. How about you?"

This felt like a fucking Ossie and Harriet movie the way we were speaking. I felt like saying, *"Look bitch, you puked. I feel like shit, so just call me a taxi and fuck off,"* but being the nice guy gentleman that I am, I of course didn't say that. Even though in hangover conditions I generally have the tendency to act none too pleasant.

You know, it's all kind of like the James Bond movies, *"Bond, James Bond."* Remember how like back in the sixties and seventies when he wanted something from a bitch, or didn't dig them, he would just slap them up. Then maybe a little later on in the flick he would be lustfully warm all over their form. Then came all this wife beating bullshit, liberation, and the like. And, it was just no longer acceptable and politically correct to do that. I mean, the times they are a-changing, and you just gotta hold your emotions and be nice—even sometimes when you just don't fucking feel like being nice.

She went for the move again.

"I wonder why I don't throw up from the Junk?"
"Because you're such a man."

Fuck, I thought what bedroom bull shit.

She ran her fingers through my hair, pulled at it just a little; as oh so sensually as possible. Possible for her that is. She was pulling my hair, kissing my cheek, going for my neck.

"You have such beautiful long blond hair."
"Sorry, I have to go to the bathroom."

I got up, headed for the head. Closed the door behind me. Locked it.

I stood there making myself hang one. I even tried to make myself sick, wondering why I wasn't.

I was trying to figure the best way out of the situation. I could have loved her, I thought. I could have, but...

Time was ticking—I was intensely aware of it. I didn't want to make it look obvious, but where was my ticket out?

Exit, into the bedroom. Patricia, minus her clothing. The bed, white. The body, white. The pussy, bushy, (actually bushy—just the way I like them).

"Come here, Stewart."
"I'm really not feeling very well."
"If I was Rosie I bet you would come over here. What's the matter with you? Aren't white girls, your own kind, good enough for you?"

Her voice was rising; she was rising, from the bed that is. She grabbed her bedspread—the white one, you know, wrapped it around her. She continued to yell.

"Or is it that you are in love with Rosie. Oh that's it! That's a fine thing! You are in love with a fucking whore!"

Now, I was beginning to get pissed. I could have really exploded, given her one of the old James Bond slaps. But, I chilled.

"How many men does she fuck a night before you get to stick it in?"
"Look Patricia, that's not nice. She's your friend too."
"She's no mutha' fucking friend of mine!"

The violence in her voice now led its way to tears.

"I am just a little sick, Patricia."
"Yeah sure. What's the matter, am I too fat for you?"
"No you're not fat at all. I'm just not feeling very sexual."
"You're such a fucking liar!"
"I could love you Patricia."

With this, she sits back down and begins to cry. An obvious ploy. An obvious maneuver—it had been used before on me. It has been used since.

The babes, when the yelling no longer gets them their desired end, they resort to the tears.

Like a fool, I sat down and put my arm around her.

"Come on Patricia, you're my buddy."
"Then why don't you act like it? Why don't you come and see me? Why won't you make love to me?"

It's like that feeling again where you just want to tell it to them straight like, *"Look bitch. I just come and hang out with you when I haven't got anything better to do or any better place or be or babe to be with."* You know like, *"Fuck you and fuck off."* Then you give them the pimp slap. You know, two or three times back and forth across the face. Then you bail out. That would be a real man's action. But, oh yeah, a modern self-actualized, no limit, secure individual would never do something so Neanderthal and macho as that.

I knew that she was going to keep sitting there bitching and crying and feeling unloved, unwanted. So, as not to damage her ego further and to dispense with the further formalities, my back was against the wall, as it were. I had to unsheathe the sword.

As I begin kissing her, her tears they stopped. Yet, as my tongue moved its way upon her face I could taste the residual saltiness.

She moved right to the stance of missionary position, vaginal intercourse intersection. I mean, she lay down on her back and pulled me on top.

As our bodies exchanged exploratory motions, I had this rather sorrowful sensation come over me. Almost the feeling as if I were cheating on my virginal, pure, and perfect lover. The feeling brought such sadness over me; I almost wanted to cry.

I don't know, maybe it was the Junk, maybe it was Thailand, maybe it was love, but my feelings for Rosie certainly were confused. She was out there every evening doing what she did best. And me, in there, inside—feeling guilty; feeling like I was cheating—cheating on a whore.

Usually it was me who was out on the outskirts. Out and cheating on all the women so loyal and true. But she was a whore and me ... I don't know, confused no doubt.

*   *   *

and the winds they blow
and the river they flow
displaced
anyplace
put me there
and there I will be

and the mystics they know
and the distance it grows
words that dance on my soul

perhaps that's the reason
perhaps that's why there's a need for lies
perhaps that's why we run
perhaps, I don't know

and every time I run away
everywhere I go
I am chased by the warriors of passion
I am chased by the mansions of sin

run and hide
run and cry
no way out
proves to be no way in

and in the distance
there is a messenger
in the distance
all is promised
in the distance
there always must be new freedom
in the distance
there lives new lies

and the winds they blow
and the rivers they flow
distance it is so much fucking easier

*   *   *

It took all I had to get the mighty pupster to fly even half-mast, though Patricia was doing her best job of tugging at it. Finally, with a mighty dispensing blow it was driven home.

Driven home—driven into her. As deeply as it would go in a half-mast position. She was full on soup. Her beaver was wet: wide, big. I mean it had given birth to a child and obviously hadn't had too much exercise of late.

Her pussy, it was like others, others of her gender and weight: gender and weight, and appetite for meals, appetite for the powder, and other addictions nondescript: big, stinky. I did my best to give her a show but it took all I had to keep from going soft.

Patricia, for all her lethargy due to the Junk was a grinder on her backside. She did huff and puff, arching her hips up and down. Me, I did my part doing what was necessary to give her a reasonable facsimile of what she thought she wanted and desired. She jelled her cookies; mine were frozen solid.

"That was good Stewart. The best ever."

I thought if she thought that was good she should see me in full proud form. Then I remember she was a liar with the tears. So, what was true? What was false? I guess, I never knew.

Done with my duty, I pulled my pants up. ...They never being completely taken off.

"I'm going to go home now."
"Oh, don't you want to stay and have breakfast and then make love some more?"
"No, I've got some things I've got to do today."
"Like what?"

She was pulling the string on my lie.

"You know, artist things."
"Oh, then you'll come back again tonight. We can do the pong kow together again."
"Well, I'll try."

I was out the door—across the planks that covered the tall Thai grass. A quick, *"Surwahdee,"* to one of the maids as I passed through the main house. When I got to the front door I saw Patricia's mother out of the corner of my eye, coming down from the second story. To avoid explanations, I just pretended not to notice and headed out.

The air was still a bit cool. I had forgotten my watch at Rosie's a week or so before, so I didn't really know what time it was. Who cares anyway?

Patricia's house was off the beaten track, as stated, so I had to hike a bit in search of a taxi to drive me home. I came upon one that the driver dude was sleeping in it. I asked for a ride. He told me to fuck off in Thai. I told him the same and hoofed on. Finally, on a main street I grabbed a *Tuk Tuk* and was headed home.

Up the stairs into the flat, it was a mess. I hit the refrigerator, no beer on hand. No beer, no coke. Fuck it, I grabbed the remainder of the vodka, left over from Rosie's and my last love convocation. I unscrewed the cap. I saw that there was still lipstick on the bottle. *"Fuck," "Can't get away from her."* I pounded it hard. Three big gulps, it was, shall we say, history.

I aimed for the bed, made it. Looked at the clock over to one side, it was only 9:30 in the A.M. What an ungodly hour. I rolled over; I saw one of Rosie's dark hairs on the brown sheets. I began to think—then I realized, *"I was in no mood to think."* I went to sleep.

Chapter 7

I awoke, my eyes opened. I was confronted by another one of those dark Asian hairs in front of my field of vision. I rolled over.

I looked at the clock, 4:12 flashed in digital red lights. I looked out my window, still daylight. 4:12 P.M. I concluded.

I did my general laying around, trying to find a reason to pull myself out of bed. Thoughts, though I tried to run from them, they continued to come to my mind. Finally, about an hour later, out of the soul sack I got; hit the showers, while a brew of the bad Thai Java was percolating.

The shower done, the Java down, and nowhere left to run: art, creativity it came to mind; somewhat as a last resort. I cranked on the tunes, went into my bedroom studio. In no mood to deal with life, I just pulled down one of the very large semi dry painting that hung from my wall and threw it on the floor. Then I sloppily staple gunned another piece of the canvas up and got into the so-called art.

I had a distance. I painted the distance. It was dark, sinister, and vague. I felt no light. It wasn't that I was really sick—hung over and/or any of the feelings in between. I just was—but was not. Very Zen, huh?

I had slapped on some paint, got a good percentage of it on me. Oil paint, that poison. The breath of its fumes is deadly. Its touch is toxic. Killing one's self slowly. But, hey, what is art all about anyway.

The side of the LP I had put on was over. I went to change it. My hands were full of paint. I reached and turned it to the other side. I realized my folly too late. I had gotten paint all over it.

I took the record; enraged, I threw it across the room smashing it on a wall. *"God damn it!"* I screamed. Then, I was mad at myself. My record collection in Thailand, none too complete, and Thailand not being on the cutting edge of music, local replacement of the album would be near impossible. *"Fuck!"* I kicked the stand which my stereo occupied sending it and the whole system flying.

I went into the bathroom, washed my hands, face, and other paint exposed parts of my body. I then, literally, ripped my painting shirt off, pulled my painting pants down. I needed a *mutha' fucking* beer or something.

As I walked back across my living room to get additional clothes to put on, I realized that I had tracked oil paint across the floor. I must of, somehow, got paint on my feet.

I was really pissed. You know, no matter how much you fucking try, it is fucking impossible to paint in an apartment and not spread the colors all over the fucking place. Though I had done it before, tried my best to clean it up, the stains perpetuated my carpet. I hated it. I was so angry at the limitation of my life. I was out the door.

As I hit the street: the Thai heat, the Thai smell, the Thai dirt smacked me back. I wanted to fight. I wished that there was a nearby bar, a nearby liquor store, anything with any availability of an intoxicating substance or some punk that I could knock the shit out of. But there was none. For that, I would have to catch a ride.

I finally got a taxi after walking about two or three blocks. I had the driver take me to this little center of illicit activities, *The Chao Praya II.* He tried to give me the rap, *"Do you need a woman?"* and all that shit but I was in no mood. I told him I didn't speak English or Thai.

*   *   *

I got out of the taxi, two stepped it into the whorehouse of choice. There they were. One hundred of the most beautiful women in the world, sitting behind a glass wall. All wearing a number. Take your choice...

Me, I always get a bit of stir when I walk in. I mean, I guess it's my long blonde hair and all. Not too many of my breed enter these realms of the abyss, I suppose... So, a little convo. can be heard behind the glass. A wave or two, a point or three, *"Take me, take me."*

I looked around a bit and there she was: a girl, beautiful, light skinned, shoulder length hair. She didn't even acknowledge my presence. Cool...

She reminded me of my Chinese babe back in L.A. The one I had left to trip here on the wild side.

I looked at her number. Walked up to the dude who controlled the microphone. He called it out. She moved in my direction. Our eyes met, literary destiny was sealed.

She took my hand. We walked towards the elevator. The thought came to me, *"Why was I going for a chick who looked so much like my babe back in L.A.?"* I don't know, maybe it was my attempting to hold on to something, anything that had some stability to it. But, why her, she was such a total Psycho Bitch. I decided to quit thinking and just get laid.

We went up the elevator into the dark realms of the abyss. We were met, as is always the case; the young maid; probably too young or too ugly to actually be a whore. She escorted us to our room.

Now, for a little urban geography here—Chao Praya II is this big massive structural complex, no windows on the outside to speak of. So, it was obviously designed and built with one specific purpose in mind—fucking to the eyes of no one. It's maybe five or six stories high and is set back from the road a bit, separated by a large parking lot.

Inside, there are long hallways lined with room. Inside of each: a couch, a coffee table, a bed, and a bathtub.

We went in, her and I. She asked as to my preference of drink. In these places I always pass—as you never know what you'll be dished up... She ordered orange juice.

Within moments the sweet young Thai maid of a whorehouse servant returned. We, the whore and I, sat upon the couch making the small talk that life is made of—zero in a zero world. She was twenty-six, I came to be told. I was older. She came from the hill country; not sold into this den of iniquity as so many of her compatriots were but made a choice to be there. Hummm, interesting...

She had a smoke; a drink of the O.J., then asked if I was ready to bathe. Now, this is a Thai whorehouse tradition, they always give you at bath before the fuck. She began to run the water; she slipped off her clothes. Her body, small, firm, perfect, like her breasts. Her beaver, like so many Thais, partially haired.

I took off my clothes, laid them upon the couch. Walked to the tub. Climbed in.

Now here I suppose I should do a little travel guide sort of thing. It's really up to the individual chick if she is going to get in the bath with you or not. Some do—some do not. Some you can persuade. Most, if they don't want to, there is nothing that you can do to entice them. This one, jumped right in.

I mean, I cannot tell you how sensuous it is. To be bathed in a bathtub by a chick that you just meet. I mean no questions asked. She was in, softly, caressingly soaping me up.

Again, back to the travel guide... Some Thai whores, try to jack you off with the soap while you're in the tub—get you in, get you off before you can really think about it. Those, you have to hit with a firm, *"No-go."* I mean, hey, you're after the pussy, aren't you?

This one was not like that. It was all softly elegant. The soaping was done. The bath was over. She pulled the plug, let the water run down the drain. She turned on the water again, tested it for its warmth. She sprayed me down with the little rubber shower thing.

We got out. She dried me off. Taking a special precaution to making sure Dick was nice and dry.

She led me towards the bed. A bed surrounded by mirrors. Now, it has always been my assumption that there is someone back there with a video camera, making free-bee porno movies for the eyes of the world. I have been told, however, that there is just a dude or thirty back there, making she that the bitches don't get slapped around or iced. But, one way or the other, who really cares?

She lay her naked Thai form down upon the bed. It was time for Dick to get hard. As she pulled me towards her, it did not take much.

In whorehouses, there's no kissing going on. No kissing more than the most elemental of pecks. So, there is never any action going to go on in that direction. The will play insistently with your dick, however. As she was doing that, and I, licking her boobs, I realized I had to go and grab a rubber.

I got up, dead-ending the movement in motion. Grabbed my pants, took out my wallet, pulled out a Trojan from inside.

Prior to putting on my condom, I realized that this was one of those whores who obviously didn't care if I wore one or not. …Makes me think that she was already infested. That, and with all the diseases around, on the travel guide side of the picture, you really need to wear one.

Dick hard, rubber on, I move back to her—skin on skin. She is lying on her back. I lay on top. She takes my cock, sticks it inside of her. The movement is again in motion. I began to gyrate.

Now, I don't know about you, but there is this thing I do—expect to do. That is to get a whore to cum. I mean some are there for just that. They figure they are fucking and may as well get off. Others are too stone cold cemented to even think of such a thing. But me, I have to give it my best shot.

So, I up and downed her relatively tight Thai pussy, then I decided, let's pay a new game. I rolled her over on top. She immediately went into action—moving, grooving.

I looked up at her as her seeming passion flourished, and there she was staring into the mirror. She was watching every move she made—looking deeply into her own eyes—in love with her self.

This did little for me. *"Fuck that, this was my dime."* I again took the bull by the horn and rolled her over onto her side. I pulled out, flipped one of her legs up and re-entered, thorough the backside style. With this, I could reach her clit with my hand—massage as necessary.

My dick moved in and out, as my fingers did the walking. But there was nothing. She was ice.

As I lay there hitting her in the fashion, my mind wandered, went to Rosie. *"Fuck, I didn't want to think of her!"* I lay there humping, thinking how this bitch could be Rosie, just another dick for another dollar, or a Thai Bhat, as it were.

With this, and the girls seeming ambivalence to what was going on. I pulled out, climbed back on top and put a hard fucking to her. I mean like, real violence it terms of a massive hard-core fuck. Bam, Bam, Bam, my cock, my body slammed into hers.

Post her screaming for pleasure filled mercy, I blew off my rocks. Well, that was that. I paid my fee. Hit the bricks. Another one bites the dust...

Chapter 8

I'm out on the street again. First thing, up comes this Thai loser of a dude and asked me if I wanted to come to his house and meet his sister,

"She's very beautiful."
"Fuck off," I told him.

I went to a liquor type store, not like we have here in the States, of course, a Thai style liquor store. I grabbed me three sixers and two bottles of Vodka. And, after getting hit up by three different pimps who offered to get me a beautiful and clean woman and a hooker or thirty who tried to pull me into their nightclub by the arm, I got a Taxi and headed back for my crib—where, though I didn't really want to be either, I thought some marginal element of peace may be found.

As we drove, the Bangkok traffic was kicking. The taxi had no air conditioning. The windows were open. The driver taking the most stupid and fucking congestion filled route he could have possibly chosen. I told him in Thai, that he was going the wrong way and that he didn't know how to drive. Now Thais, having more than an aggressive persona, he told me that I was wrong and that how could a *falong* know Bangkok or how to drive this city better than him. I was on the verge of just getting out of the god damned taxi as it sat, dead stopped, in the full-on pollution and the ear shattering noise of the Bangkok traffic zone. *"I could walk fucking faster than this,"* I thought. But, I knew there would be no easy ride home from my current position, so I just cracked open a bottle of the liquid passion, vodka, kicked back and drank it down as went nowhere fast.

By the time I got back to my pad I had killed about half the bottle. I paid the driver the meter money but gave him no tip, which obviously pissed him off by the look on his eyes. *"Good. Fuck you,"* I thought.

It was dark by the time I got there. But Bangkok, it did still smell bad.

Inside my apartment, the digital display flashed 7:13. I sat down on my couch in the dark, cracked a brew open and one sipped the bad pup. I followed through with a few more.

I could not help but breathe the paint fumes. They were especially potent in the dark. I could see my stereo lying on the floor. I wonder if it was broken, I didn't even fucking care.

The smell inside, outside. The heat. There was no place to run. *"Man, I'm no better off here than I was in L.A,"* I thought. *"No place to really paint, no fully creative space where I didn't have to worry about the carpets or the walls. No place that I can go where my sense of smell is not destroyed by oil paint fumes. Why the fuck am I even here, when I could be living back in L.A.?"*

Back in L.A. where the heat is at least tolerable and the winters are cool. And besides, there's even a lot of Thai babes in the city now. I know I could find one. And she wouldn't even be a whore like Rosie.

Rosie, there was that thought again. Was that why I was pissed off? Rosie, did I love her that much like Patricia said?

Patricia, I could go to her house. I could get high. I could get laid. That's it, that's what I'll do...

I hammered one more beer for the road. Stashed an unopened bottle of the vodka in a brown paper bag, and with it in hand, hit the road—the hard road.

Outside, I quickly grabbed a taxi. As it drove to Patricia's, the Bangkok traffic was still heavy but the cab was air-cooled. The driver, he was gazing in his rear-view mirror as I wet my lips with the bottle in question. We drove on. I drank on, thinking thoughts that I did not wish to think.

Was Patricia home? She was a bit of a flake. Was she stoned when the invitation was placed, table center?

Rosie… a whore… Could I really be that in love with a whore? I thought I had kept my love distance. Not laying my jugular open to attack. And where the fuck was she? She had not contacted me for four days now. She had done that before but not after such a close session like the one we had with the Junk. Yeah, that's it; I am goddamned angry with her. *"Yeah,"* I said it out loud as the driver drove on, probably thinking I was some crazy fucking *falong.* Well, fuck him too.

*   *   *

Knock, knock.

"Surwahdee."

One of the maids answered the door. Directed me to the back house. Yes, she was home. I walked, or should I say, staggered on.

"Bringing your own?"

I hear the voice speak to me in French. Patricia's mother.

I look at her, what answer could I give?

"Oui, mademoiselle."

I laughed, I staggered on. I move from the cool to the heat. I sauntered across the wooden planks. I would breathe deep but the Bangkok air, is no-go. I knocked, fuck it, I just open the door. Inside, it's cool.

"Stewart, I thought that you weren't going to come. It was getting so late."

"What and forget you. We had a date, remember? Sorry I am late. Today was a very busy day. A lot of art to create, you know."

She walks up and plants a juicy one upon my lips.

Patricia was already high. I could tell. Looking around I saw it, the *pong kow,* laid out on the night table.

"Partying, huh?"

"Oh,   do some with me, Stewart. It's so special when we do it together. It's what brought us together; made us lovers."

"Yeah right," I thought. Just like any other fucking junky—together or alone, they do the bad stuff. Look at her, there she was surrounded by a white room, in white clothing, so fucking pure, and jacked up on the Junk all alone.

"I don't want to snort it again; my nose hasn't felt right since. Let's smoke it."

"Why Stewart, is it too intense for you?"

"Nothing is too intense for me baby."

Well, as any fool dives deeply into the bounds of desire, so did I. And never let it be said that anyone can out do me.

I bent down, leaned over the table and bap'ed a large percentage of the white particles up my nose. I sat down on her bed. She sat next to me. I remember for a second, and then I went down. I was out-a-there.

Maybe it was the booze. Maybe it was I hit too much, too hard. Maybe it was my anger. Maybe it was the heat. I don't know.

*　　*　　*

"I was worried about you."

I awoke gradually. My first vision was Patricia over the table with a straw in her nose. I could tell that she was really worried ...

"How long was I out?"
"Maybe half an hour."

I sat up. I was still on, my head spun. I lay back down. Patricia rolled over on top of me—not an easy weight to take. She began kissing my cheeks, my neck. She unbuttoned my shirt, began kissing my chest.

She moved down, slowly down—zipper down. She began to kiss my dick. My brain was too shattered to fight back or even give a flying fuck.

"Do you love me Stewart?"
"Don't talk with your mouth full."

To my surprise, I rose to attention. All systems were go! She let her lips do the talking. Soon she was undressing herself.

My head still spun. My body, however, yearned.

Now no one ever denies that sex relieves tension. No one ever denies it, no one ever will; except maybe some bull shit message from God sort of nightlife preacher.

As she rose her body atop mine: insertion, gyration, the force began to grow; the weight just a bit too god damned heavy. I rolled her over, began to power stroke.

I was angry. Angry like I was at the whore. Angry that I was there, fucking this Godzilla of a woman. Angry, that I once thought she was my friend, (men and women can never be friends). Angry that I was in Thailand with nothing to go home to. Angry at that fucking whore Rosie.

The thought of Rosie made me fuck harder and harder. Patricia began to scream.

I gave Patricia the power pile driver. I felt Patricia's arms tightly around me. I pulled lose, lifted my body up as I continued to fuck. I looked at her obesity, her boobs, stretch marked and hanging, her flab moving with my movement. I was not turned on. I was just fucking. Fucking someone who I had thought was my friend. Fucking someone who I had even believed I could love. I was wrong.

Her body fat moved—her first cum, was cuming. She was noisy, she was sloppy; not like—no, not like Rosie.

"Damn it, why can I not stop thinking about her, even as I am making love to another woman!" Her body doesn't have flab. Her breasts have no stretch marks.

Rosie ...

I kept fucking Patricia but my mind was on Rosie. Rosie, I could not stop thinking about her! I thought of making love to her. I thought of her body. I thought...

For a moment, I was so lost in the dreams of her and I together; it was as if I were making love to her. Me, the one who swore to never fantasies about another woman while fucking the closest one at hand. Me, I never had a fantasy like this before. Rosie, you goddamn whore, I love you!

The fantasy shatter as Patricia's nasal panting rang in my ear. She held me tight, too tight, not sensually tight like Rosie. I fucked. I fucked hard. I was fucking out of anger. The anger at the goddess, the goddess of Siam. She had slammed dunked me again. Set me up, reeled me in, like a fish. Set me up, set me in the love motion with a whore who I did not even know where she was; probably fucking someone else. The anger made me still fuck harder. I wanted to cum. I needed to cum. To show Rosie I didn't need her. To feel that momentary no-thing-ness. To communicate with the gods. To tell them that they were once again fucking me over, fucking around with my head, not giving me valid choices; with life, as it is, being lived in terms of availability.

I fucked harder. I tried to cum. I tried hard. Patricia had dried up. I had no choice but to stop.

As she was falling off to drug induced, sex induced sleep,

"You're the very best ever Stewart."

*   *   *

Morning so sweet in its passion, so warm in its caress, so all knowing; full of so much love. The morning, this particular morning, the morning then, it came on none too sweet.

Patricia was waltzing around her one room cottage. The noise of her movement, being the light sleeper that I am, awoke me. Awoke; death it may have been a better alternative. I was sick as a *mutha' fuck'n* dog.

The formalities were exchanged. Patricia in love dosage heaven. Me, the Junk and the fluid mixed explosively once again.

Patricia wanted to take a shower. I wanted to die. She took her shower. I faded back into the restless haze of a hangover sleep.

Out of the shower, she jumped on the bed.

"I love you Stewart. Let's get high."

Love the passion of a dreamer. Junk the desire of a fool. Mixed there can be no winners. Separate there is only room for their perpetual fantasies.

"No fucking way."
"Why are you sick? I'm not."

116

I tried to roll over, cover my head with a pillow, and hide my soul from the world. As the movement was in motion I noticed the clock, non-digital ticking time. I hate ticking! It was a little after 8:00 A.M.

Now this was fucking early. I scanned my mind and realized that we had probably gone to sleep at about ten or so, but eight fucking o'clock...

Patricia tried to kiss me. I was in no mood.

"Do some pong kow with me Stewart. It'll make you feel better."
"No way am I ever going to touch that fucking dog food ever again."
"Dog food, what is dog food?"
"Dog, you know, we call pong kow that in the States," I struggled to say.
"Oh, ha ha. Dog or dog food. That's very funny."

She sat there laughing.

"Stewart, why do they call it that?"
"Fuck off..."

My head hurt, my mind spun. I did not want to talk. I did not want to answer questions. She kept rap'n on.

"Patricia, just leave me the fuck alone. I am very sick."

*   *   *

and the moments
they cast their thoughts to surrender
the dreams they die
on the battlefield of lost love
life, it survives
in a space filled with far less than glory

and the morning cries for its screams to be heard.

vision is lost
to encroaching desire
enlightenment
to thoughts of lust
illusion will demand its way
and human nature will allow it to be heard

if there was nothing
then nothing would be the norm
but here, in this space
in this time
in this century
there is everything
it all can be had

having been seen
having been touched
desire is the course of the day

once it is felt
once it is held
all that one wants
is simply to run away

nothing to nothing
all to all
and the wind it will still blow
the rain it will still fall
and the dreams of wanting
will turn to the desire for running
until it has all gone away

*   *   *

Finally, in all her consideration Patricia left the room and turned off the T.V. which she had so consciously let blast into my ears in Thai dialect. She left me to sleep, or to more accurately lie there in the density of hang over pain.

"Never, never, never again," I repeated to myself.

*   *   *

Now, I am not going to try to explain the pains and evils of the one too many to you, whatever that one too many may be. But, I will take this moment to say that I was seriously latched up.

As I rolled in and around Patricia's king-sized bed trying to hide from myself but finding nowhere to run, I wondered, as all fools do, why I had let myself become entangled in the roots of the demon. Once again lost with no apparent way out of the maze. The fucking story of my life.

My mind went to a time not too many years the previous. It was a bar; my buds Saturday Jim and Vincenzo's grandmother had checked out. The wake; an Italian wake, held at a cocktail lounge of her son. Drinking it was a way to hide the tears that came to the eyes.

We stopped in for a moment, a moment that turned into three. We stopped in for a glass of remembrance, a mourning that took far too tight a hold. One drink of the Jack led to three, four, five.

The uncle, the son, wanted the world to know he still had a tight muscular stomach, *"Hey Stewart, give me a few of those karate chops you know how to do in the old breadbasket."* I drunkenly gave him many. He had to hurt the next day. The next day after his wedding day; for in all his anguish, all his methods of running from and to, he at the age of late forty something had gotten married for the first time in his life that day, the day after his mother had died.

Saturday Jim and I we drank hard, we drank heavy. Vincenzo, had too tight of a hangover, chilled and just hung tight—hung out, one sipping a brew or two.

I bought him a drink. He didn't drink it. I threw it on him. He should have knocked me out. He should have, but we were buddies. And he, being a serious party man himself, saw how I was aced big time. He should have knocked me out; it would have saved us all a lot of trouble.

Saturday Jim and I, we were way full on. By the bathroom was a tray of tuna sandwiches. Saturday Jim is allergic to the fish of the sea. I was a cold monk, I told him they were made of chicken salad. He drunkenly ate them. He began to puke big time.

Two or three bottles of the bad Jack later we were on our way out. I do not remember leaving the bar. I remember being in the pick-up truck I owned at the time. I riding shotgun, Saturday Jim at the helm, Vincenzo, riding *negro;* center-spot. We got on the freeway, we began puking our guts; Saturday Jim and I—all over the inside of the truck. Vincenzo got puked all over. Like a real man, he took it in stride.

It was off the freeway Saturday Jim way too fucked up to drive. He got off, and then tried to get back on. Get back on—entering on the off ramp. I remember the horns and the head on traffic coming. He hung a U'y mid ramp.

We were off again. He was fucked up. I was worse. He had been drinking and puking, due to the tuna fish sandwiches. Me, the Jack initially hung tight. Vincenzo hung—sober, straighter than either of us—straighter but didn't know how to drive a stick shift.

I don't remember much. I didn't remember it then. Saturday Jim had pulled over to take a rest. We were sitting on the grass, the grass of somebody's expensive lawn. I decided to leave—drive off into the sunset, drive to the arms of my main L.A. babe lover, a Spanish girl, long lost—long forgotten. Drive to where I would be safe and protected.

I got in the truck, so I am told. I drove away. Saturday Jim hung on the side trying to jump in the passenger window, trying to get the keys, trying to get me to stop. I drove on laughing like a mad man. I sideswiped an expensive imported car or two, in this high level suburban L.A. neighborhood, trying to get the bad dude off.

I did, I drove. I remember being on the freeway. I remember smacking a mobile home in a traffic jam. I remember dodging traffic to bail out of that tourist's field of vision. I remember that. Then it was Culver City, Sepulveda Boulevard, a cop I could see the lights flashing in my mirror.

I was on the streets, trying to get home. Trying to get somewhere where I would be protected. Trying to be somewhere where I would be safe. Trying to get to the arms of main L.A. babe. I should never have done her so wrong so many times. Trying, but I did not make it.

My hands out the window...

"You got me officer, I'm fucked up."

He drove me to the station. I puked in his car. I was amazed he didn't kick my drunken ass for that. At the station, they took my possessions; let me make one phone call.

I was so drunk they put me in a padded cell.

The drunken moments tick by. They tick by so slow when you are not where you should not be, not where you want to be. And sobering is so fucking hard when the sickness in coming on strong. No different than here, no different than there; Bangkok.

My main L.A. babe came and picked me up, picked me up in a little red MG I had bought for her. I should have loved her better. She definitely deserved better than me. Finding a better man than I was, I guess that is not hard.

She picked me up, cleaned me up, and even drove home my pick-up truck. The one I had driven. The one I had smashed. The one we had puked all over. The one the officer had left the lights on, the windows down, and my wallet full of credit cards and three hundred dollars cash lying on the front seat floor. Yes, I should have been far better to her.

That was then. I was sick, sick for a week. Thought I had cracked a piston. Paranoid, that I had killed someone. Scared that the police would come any day and arrest me. I could not remember much of anything.

Then, Bangkok, that was then too—the sick, the drug sick, the alcohol sick. Had I not learned anything? No, I had not. I was still this Bohemian mystic who lost himself years ago in India and only a partial shell of a man returned.

The bed spun. It continued to spin even as the day went on. I tried to sleep, no-go. I tried a shower, no help. I even listen to the radio, big uck. I desired a hangover sized soft drink bottle of the 7-Up variety. The kind I used to get back in L.A. every Saturday night, 4:00 A.M.ish, when the punk music was going strong and it had been a full-on weekend. I wanted one but was far too involved in my invalidness to get up and get one.

*   *   *

It must have been four or five o'clock in the evening. I don't know, maybe I was feeling a bit better; maybe... Patricia had not returned, and I must admit that the thought of her not falling all over me and taking care of me did upset me more than a bit. *"Fucking self-involved junky,"* I thought.

Even though I was still a bit intoxicated and feeling none too chipper, I pulled it out, out-a-bed. Got dressed and hit the planks which led to the house, which led to the sidewalks, which led to the back streets of Bangkok.

The maid, *"Surwahdee,"* hands clasped in prayer position. I was in no mood, I just headed on out.

Outside, it was to my amazement that a taxi cruise'n by oh so empty awaited my beckoned call. *"Thank you,*

God." Even the air conditioning worked. A quick stop for some hang over juice, carbonated soda and I was home.

It was almost dark; the smell of paint seemed more than unpleasant. The stereo still lay on the floor. The thought once again came to my mind, is it broken? I left it for another time to find out what condition its condition was in.

When I left the last time, I had not left the air conditioning on, which provoked me more than a little. So, it was hot when I re-entered. I turned it on.

On the couch; leave the lights off, the soda went down good. The air conditioning kicked in. I lay there in that oblivion that is only known to those who have attempted a trance with the *soma,* the intoxicating substances of the world. Attempted the trance, a trance that can never last. No, it never does. I lay there wishing it were some other place, some other time, some other feeling; anything, anything.

*   *   *

Pushing 9:00 P.M., on the hard side, I couldn't get the thought of Rosie out of my mind. I hadn't seen her in four days and though I wished my physical condition would have been in less dangerous waters, my emotions in less hazardous straights, I changed into some cleaner duds and out into the heat I went with Rosie's apartment in mind.

My ride was a *Tuk Tuk.* The night time air still hot, undoubtedly fuelled by the passion that burns rampant in the Bangkok brothels in the dead of the night.

The drive full of indecision, full of wonder, whether Rosie would even be there. Or would she be there alone?

I arrived at her place. It was like the first time, two months the previous. The same hesitation, the same doubt existed. Should I go up the stairs? Should I go to the door? I, as I had done previously had to walk the block a time or two before I made my move.

I knew that I was in no mood to deal with any unsavory situation. I knew it and thought that the inevitable would happen and I would probably have to blaze some punk up. Had it not been for the nausea that I was feeling, had it not been for intoxication I had been experiencing, had it not been for the dagger sharp question that Patricia had asked me regarding my love for a whore, I don't think I would have made the assent of the stairs at all. But, I found myself at the door.

"Stewart!"

Hugs met my presence.

"I've missed you."

Lipstick kisses met my lips. Ah, lipstick kisses...

"Are you alone?"
"Of course, I am alone, silly. Come in."

I was in.
Sitting down I was embraced by my love, the love of a whore; love none the less. My heart, you know that feeling, began to soar, like a thousand needles in a voodoo doll in Haiti. Yes, it was love.

"So, Stewart, where have you been?"

Rosie asked me with a smirk on her face.

"Where have you been?"

I rebounded her question.

"Guess who came to see me here today."

124

"Who?"
"Oh Stewart, you've been a naughty boy."
"Huh?"
"Come on Stewart, guess who was here today."
"I don't want to guess. I'm sick. Come on, tell me who."
"I know you're sick, you bad boy."

I knew what was coming but did not want to hear the words that were going to be spoken out of her mouth.

"Come on guess."
"Stop fucking around, just tell me!"
"Oh, you're no fun. I'm not going to tell you."
"Fine, don't."

I knew that would play her.

"Okay, Okay, Patricia came today."
"Patricia?"
"Yes, and she told me all about you two."
"Told you what?"
"That now you were hers and I couldn't come and see you anymore."

With that, the happy expression on her face faded. I could see tears forming in her eyes. Her eyes, eyes that never cried. Then all of a sudden it was back to the joke.

"So you did pong kow with her, yes?"
"Yes, but..."
"If you love her why'd you come here to me?"
"Now wait a minute! I didn't say any of that, she did!"

Inside I was way angry, mega pissed off that Patricia would do something so bull shit as that. It was just fucking like her, I thought.

"But she's falong like you. I understand, you want to be with your own kind."

"That's the farthest fucking thing from the truth. I hate falong women. Why do you think I have come to Asia all these times, all these years? Why do you think Rosie?"

"I know Stewart, all of your talk of taking me to America was just bed talk. I hear it all the time. You think I'm just a prostitute. I know you don't really love me."

"Yes, I do god damn it. I do love you."

I couldn't believe those words came so firmly out of mouth.

"Yes, I love you Rosie. And I never said anything about America, you did. I don't even want to be there."

Now, the moments and the memory of the words fade into obscurity with the fullness of the embrace she gave me upon the completion of my statement. Other things were said, reiterations I believe, explanations for sure, lies no doubt. But the kiss, the touch, the feeling, is what I remember in exacting detail.

I made love to her that night. I made love with her. Her golden Asian body next to mine. Her skin so soft, so perfect. Her breasts, so firm. No excess weight anywhere. Just the pulsation of the muscles, my muscle of love.

The night proceeded in its own perfection. Somehow, I have no remembrance of the hangover. Somehow all I can remember is the love.

Chapter 9

Morning woke in its afternoonness as it does in the perfection of my style, my perfect world. I awoke there she was in all her Thai beauty, her naked glory—Rosie, leaning over me, staring at me. Gazing with the look of her loving eyes. There could be no more of a heavenly way to awake.

Love was made. Words were spoken. Afternoon saw us eating breakfast in this little semi-secluded Thai cafe. Return to her apartment. Again, love was made. Again, words were spoken.

The evening fell softly upon me as it was decided to once again indulge in the powder that opened the gates of the gods.

We got high, not too high, just high enough. Smoking it was way more mellow.

Ten o'clock rolled around, abruptly Rosie got up: had to leave, places to be, people to see, business to attend to. Business, a word I never wanted to know about.

"I have to pay my bills Stewart. I'm not rich like you are."

Rich, if she only knew how poor and in debt I actually was.

In a seeming instant she was gone, out the door, down the stairs. I was alone, assured that it was fine if I wished to stay there all night, I could.

No, I was not going to stay there all night! I was alone. I was angry. I was high.

I left. I went out. In the distance, a voice it called to me. Yes, it was a voice. I could hear it vaguely, yet definitely. It was the far away voice of revenge. Out the door, huh? We'll see about that. Let's get even.

Now *get even*—it can take on many forms. I mean this is Bangkok. But with the lack of motivation, the lack of the desire which the *pong kow* brings on, I decided that the easiest formation of revenge, which the little voice spoke of, would be to just go over and get a little higher and power thump Patricia.

That is one of the things about getting high; you always want to get higher.

As I rode over in a taxi complete with no air conditioning, I thought to myself that I really should be more creative with this vengeful situation. I mean I should go and put the pupster to one of Rosie's night time princess friends. I mean that would really get her back, right? But the desire to go seeking a whore who knew her was just not there.

Pain, that's what I was feeling. Pain, so that's what I wanted to cause. Would Rosie even care?

On the way, in time and in place, I stopped off for a bottle of my preferred poison. Though my mind told me not to play with the double-sided venom, I, in all my intoxicatedness said, *"Fuck it,"* and a bottle of vodka I got.

Through the door, I did not feel like knocking. Over the planks, I did not look for snakes. In her room, there she was; high, like me, and getting higher. *"Damn, she must spend a lot of time in this room alone getting wasted,"* I thought.

Love and kisses were placed upon my form. I really didn't care. I cracked the bottle. Hit it hard. My nose down over the night-time candy—care to care less.

"Do you know who I saw today Stewart."

Oh, fuck, here we go again.

"No, who?"
"Rosie."
"Who?"

The story went on; Patricia's side, her version…
About that, I did not care either.

"I love you Stewart."

About that; who gives a fuck?
Sex, revenge, get even; that was what was on my
mind. Get it up. Get it in. Get it even.
I pulled the pupster out of my pants. It was already
hard. I put the play full on—lifted up her skirt, sent the dick
straight home. Her pussy was dry. Good thing it was semi
stretched out or I probably would have broken then bad boy
in half as I didn't care and shoved it in hard.

"Owh," she said. *"Take your time."*

Fuck that.
I fucked her. I didn't care. Periodically, I'd stop, pull
out, hit the bottle, and hit the Junk. I hit them hard.
Patricia found her way into the realms of sex
induced, drug induced sleep. I lay there my dick soft from
the cuming, my mind soft from the Junk, my heart frozen in
its confusion, lost in its fear.

*   *   *

and the ways to ecstasy
lead to the ways of the lost
over the hill
into a land far far away
and the dreams of the mystics
turn to the nightmares of the sane
when all the walls come a tumbling down

*   *   *

In all my macho glory, I felt more pain than fulfilment. In all my high, I felt more lost than alive. I had taken my revenge but felt no better. I had my way but nothing had been accomplished.

As I lay in Patricia's bed, trying to force myself to fall asleep, all I could think of was how had I gotten trapped by my own hanging noose, how I had let myself, once again, fall prey to my own game.

I loved. Yes, I loved a whore. How could I have let that happen? How?

Why didn't I tell her to stop what she was doing, two plus months ago? Why didn't she just stop?

Every day, every night, another man knew her form. Every day, every night another. When my dream had always been to find a virgin, a commodity that had always seem to just slip from my grasp. A virgin, a whore, a stoned California mystic in Thailand. Who was I kidding; another dick was finding its way home into her this very moment. *"I know it, I just know it!"*

The dick rules this fucking world. I am going to go and kill that *son-of-a-bitch* who is fucking the woman I love. I am!

Up, I was. Clothes, on—as best as I could put them on. Out the door: the heat, the smell, I leaned over and threw up off of Patricia's patio.

I walked onto the planks. Like a tightrope. Yes, that's what they were, a tight rope. I saw myself on one. I fell off. It took me forever to hit the ground. I felt myself falling in slow motion, like in a bad B-movies. I lay in the grass. It bled its moisture on to me. The grass, I thought. The tight rope planks, I thought. The Thai snakes. Snakes! I will die. I called to Patricia, stoned she did not come to my aid. I tried, tried hard to get up. Get away from the snakes. I tried but it was no use. I want in, the snakes were going to get me.

"Patricia!" The call to no avail. I knew they felt my body heat. They were slithering on their way to get me now. They were, I knew it. The name, the call, and I could not get up. I screamed.

The maid, the nice one. The old one. Yes, that one. I see her in the fog that covered over me that evening. I see her coming towards me. She lifted me, stood me up. No, I did not want a taxi. No snakes. I want sleep. In there. Yes, in there. I mumbled in Thai. Up the stairs she guided me. Patricia lay passed out on her bed. She had her blouse open; her dress pulled up, pussy very exposed. I want in there, I continued to mumble.

Inside the guesthouse, inside the room; drugs had been taken, drugs had been consumed. Drugs, they were evident. Did the maid see them? She had to. The family had to know what was going on. Thailand, the most addicted to the powder white country in the world. They had to know.

"Yes, I'm fine," I told her and told her again.
"Go, you must go. Go-Go. Thank you, go away."

In my tracks, I fell on the floor. I saw the light dim as the door was closed behind me. I looked; I felt, was it moist? No. Good, then no snakes. I screamed out, *"Rosie,"* just once, one more time before I faded somewhere, into some realm that defies words and explanations that can never be defined. I was out, asleep. Safe, for the moment…

*　　*　　*

I was awakened by the smell of a body upon mine. Like, wake up and smell the lust. Patricia had found me; made her mark, cast her mould. Wet pussy juice, I could feel its movement upon my genital region. My pants had been pulled down.

Drugs and distance, wine and women, they all sing the same song. The movement leads to a panic; trapped, I was trapped.

I rolled over. Patricia did not find this acceptable. She tried to keep the juices flowing, up and down, back and forth. She had her body stroking whatever part of me that was within reach. She tried to turn me back around, get the pup in motion. Nailed, is what she wanted. Being French she didn't want to take no for an answer.

"Patricia, leave me the fuck alone. There is no way in the fucking world I can make love right now!"

Make love as opposed to sex. Make love as opposed to fucking. I tried to be nice. And after all, there is a difference you know in the aforementioned: style, technique, and purpose thereof.

She would not stop. Finally, I took all the energy of drained intoxication that I could muster up and pushed her off. I dragged myself from the floor as if a spell of death had taken its toll upon my body and the ethereal cord was dragging me to heaven.

"I just don't need this right now!"

I pulled my clothing on as best as possible. I would've hated to make an objective opinion of how I must have looked. The booze, the drugs, and yes, even the snakes in the grass.

My clothing on, as best as they could be all current conditions considered. My long hair hanging in whichever direction its freedom felt fit to inhabit. I tried to push it back a bit as I walked out the door into the Thai morning heat.

Across the tight rope planks, I walked. Through the house; in through the back door, if you catch my drift.

"Looks like you brought your own last night too, Stewart."

I heard a distant French voice ring in my ear. I looked, being the gentleman that I am I smiled. It was she, Patricia's mother. I was out the door, the front one this time.

I wonder had the maid told her master of the occurrences of the night before. I wondered what she had seen, what she had noticed. I wondered how a mother could let it go on under and in front of her respective nose. I wondered how even if the daughter was twenty-seven years old, in space and in time. I wondered why...

On the street it was obviously a Bangkok morning. People moved, bald Buddhist monks, beggar bowls in hand; begged. Food was being cooked. I could smell it. Me, I walked. I needed to get some place, any place, I didn't know where. A place where there was a place left to run. Something that I had lost a long time ago. I needed a place.

As I walked in pursuit of transportation, I could sense the distance, I could feel the lingering of the fluid, the enduring sensation of the Junk. Yes, it was there, yet I walked on.

I checked to make sure I was in fact walking. I wondered if I was still really alive. Maybe I had died and gone to the astral realm on the Thai side of never-never land. Alive and walking. I pinched myself just to be sure.

Moving, did I want to throw up? No. Did I want to pass out? No. In fact, I was AOK and moving on. I just wanted a place to be.

In the *Tuk Tuk* that I finally got, I could not believe that I was not devastatingly sick. No, I could not believe it. And, without a thought of purpose or presence, I was *en route* to the abode of Rosie.

pass me a glance of the passing passion
pass it to me in a beggar's bowl
give me a sign of the divine perfection
let me ride it one more time

and when all is lost
and when all is gone
and when nothing else remains
when a kiss of a whore
is all that was known
then a kiss of whore
is cast to realms of passive perfection

Night had fallen hard the evening last and I needed a brew or something to wash it down with. It had to be early; nothing was open. I looked down to check the time but my Rolex was missing. I had finally picked it up at Rosie's the night before. Did the maid take it? I didn't know but somehow it did not seem to matter very much to me.

Tuk Tuk driving, we passed a dude pushing his cart full of iced and sugared cola cans. On his way to an appropriate spot of financial distribution. I had the driver pull over. I got out with no great ease. I was definitely not riding on all cylinders. I grabbed me a cola. And though it had no alcoholic content, it did take the edge off the cottonmouth as the drive drove on.

Arriving at Rosie's, I had no problem ascending the stairs. The distance made it pure and simple. As simple as a sweet love, with a sweet bottle of wine. If some dude were there, I would just kill him. No problem. If she is not there I will just break the fucking door down. And if love and life are just right, it will all be a dream and none of her past will have ever happened and we will live happily ever after with a white picket fence.

I knocked. The door was opened for me.

"Stewart you look like shit. Have you been partying again? Come in here, let me take care of you."

Ah, subservience, how I do love it.

She undressed me, placed me in her shower: washed me, soaped me, and even kissed me more than a few times.

"Why didn't you stay here last night? I expected you to be here when I got home."

I didn't answer, though the mention of the night before plastered me into the pagan realms of the reality that I did not want to feel.

Out of the shower, into the refrigerator I hammered down a brew. The words they were spoken, but the words they just were not felt. I just said, *"Fuck it,"* to myself out loud and lay down and went to sleep.

I don't know how long I slept, a while though. I awoke to the spectrum of two loud voices speaking in Thai.

"No, he's not yours."
"Yes, he is. He's mine, you're just a whore!"
"No, he says that he loves me. And, what are you, just a mama's girls."
"Fucking keep it down," I yelled.

I yelled, but the argument continued and now I was involved. It went back and forth of who was who, what was what, and tell me who do you love. Believe me, I was in no mood.

"You fucking bitches fight it out among yourselves. I'm out-a-here."

Now, there can be little worse than being woken up—woken up in the kind of state that I was in, by that kind of violent conversation. In my semi soberness, in my drunken stupor clothes, I was on my way. And though Patricia followed me down the stairs a bit, the two of them seemed far more content to cat fight among themselves; victor take all.

I drunkenly laughed as I walked up the cemented path to my apartment building, a bottle I had picked up in hand. I laughed, a whore and a chunky French bitch, leave it to me to get involved with two women that can do nothing for me in the long run but give me heart ache and head ache and a very passing kiss of passion. The joke, as it always seems to be, was on me.

*   *   *

The bottle, I hit about one forth down and lay out on my couch. It was dark when I woke up. I couldn't see my clock, but it was still night.

I looked around my apartment, what a fucking mess. Even the smell of paint reaffirmed my failure in all areas of material life. An apartment/studio, Bangkok, and the brew. I was so messed up. I knew it.

I had no desire to be in the confines of my apartment, the reality just hit me too fucking hard. As I hit the bad bottle hard for a wakeup call, I knew it would be the one time for the road—the hard road. Still in the clothing I had worn the night and the day and the night before that, I was out, out the door.

Bangkok at night: as the neon lights flashed, as the heat poured on, as the dark goddess embraced all the lost souls of the damned. I had no desire to go searching. I had

136

no desire for answers to all my dreams. I just had a pounding feeling to go to a space where it all could be taken away.

At Patricia's house, I knocked at the door. The helpful maid from the night before welcomed me. I asked her about my watch but to no avail. *"Yeah right, I bet you took it you fucking bitch,"* I thought.

Through the door and out onto the tight rope, night rope, planks surrounded by Thai grasses and Thai snakes, I walked to the rear of the house, to Patricia's *palais de amour.* In peripheral vision, I noticed a glistening. And though it took all I had to force myself into the foliage, there I found my watch. All my feeling of knowing that the maid had taken it faded into the embrace of my own foolishness.

Patricia was all laughter and smiles.

"I knew you would choose me."

Now to tell the story, we got high—up the old nostril as she had a preference for. To continue but to keep it as concise as possible, we also; well, I was kind of forced and persuaded into it, if you know what I mean, being the wholesome, innocent, and naive person that I am, we had, how-you-say; sex.

Now, it isn't that she was all that bad in the bed department. And, it isn't that there wasn't a moment in time that I thought more of her than I actually should have. It's just that somehow illusion falls when you've been there, done that.

Sex, well, for the most part it's generally all right with me. It's not rare however, that I lose interest after the first encounter or so. And that's just about exactly what had happened with Patricia.

Patricia being French and all, the poop shoot seemed to be the placement position of paradise. And besides, I had to keep some form of interest going. So, the main line, mega dick was juiced and though she didn't expect it, when it came sex time again, I rolled her over and slid it right in.

Her backside went easy. She French, right? It was designed for such an activity. Some are, some aren't, you know. But it was a quick hop, skip, and a jump to the pleasure zone for yours truly. Her ass was way more tighter than her pussy and I had no real desire to have a prolonged put her butt to sleep session, anyway.

Patricia claimed it was her first time on the flip side/back side, taking that old dirt road. But, I don't know? I never have been one to believe the lies and words of the masses.

A long story made short, after the fuck in the ass, we proceeded to get higher.

*   *   *

I cribbed over at the pad of pleasure for the evening. Morning came and I shot my dice one more time—again asshole side. Then, I was out of there. To be perfectly frank, Rosie was on my mind.

I wasn't sick. I was still a little stoned, yes. I was still a little drunk, yes. But sick, no. I dug the feeling. I had partied down, kissed the gates of the master of illusion and was alive and walking to tell about it.

I knocked on Rosie's door.

"I knew you would choose me."

Hey, like woe, *deja vu* dude. The words they sounded similar. Had I heard them somewhere before?

Her apparent victory in the battlefield of love found my way or should I say my rod's way into her canal of love. Now I don't want to sound macho or full of myself here, but I do have to admit that though my feeling of love for her penetrated every source of my way lost subconscious being, the distance developed by the *pong kow* let other things, less important things, ring truer and truer in the far off reaches of my otherwise engaged mind.

Our love session led to our Junk session and so it went and so it goes.

Chapter 10

It was night. It was the dream, the dream that I had lost myself in. There we were, with the cold pagan pulse of the Junk flowing through our bodies like formaldehyde pulsing through the veins of the dead. We were not alone, Rosie and I. Into the picture had stepped two others. Two others, who like her, had a passion for the powder. Two, no, in fact, three counting Rosie. They had placed their vice in their arms, hammered it in like a nail of destiny. Like Jesus upon the cross, attached by a needle.

Me, stoned, drunk, I do not why I had the discretion to say, *"No."* Just say no...

I smoked it as I watched them inject it into their arms.

They were pavement princesses, blood to Rosie. Beautiful, damn, they were both beautiful. In a haze, I remember wondering why don't any of those dudes who plant their pups for a price ever really realize how way beautiful, how mega special, how too perfect these babes are. Man, it's like sad that dudes just can't see that these hookers are people too. And sure, they have learned their trade. And sure, they are messed up. Hey, we're fucked up in one way or another. And given another chance, a different destiny, they would way for sure have gone in another direction. How can you hold it against them? Dudes and their dicks—me too. What fucking assholes we are.

*   *   *

I don't know quite how it happened; the memory is so vague. I was sitting on the floor next to this beauty. I had my arm around her, telling her: if this was another place, another time, if I was not in love with Rosie, that way for sure, I would love you.

140

This dude, one of their friends had come in; initially seemed nice enough. Probably was a love punk fag. Made his bucks or his *bhat* by getting dicked in the ass. He was the one, later I was told, that Rosie had gone to score from post our session with the Thai police.

Anyway, arm around this bitch; all of a sudden it was like a knife in my stomach, then a *stiv* in my brain. I couldn't hold it back. I began to throw up. I fell, I lay face first on the floor, holding my stomach, holding my head, screaming... I could not even breathe.

Then it was like a convulsion. I felt like I was on one of those vibrating belt lose weight machines from the fifties. It was pulsing. I was turning, spinning. Life it went all red, like I was at the gates of hell.

I don't know, I guess they picked me up. I remember being under two of their arms: the guy's and this chick's. They were walking me around this crowded, smoke filled apartment. As I peered through distant hazy eyes.

"Hang on Stewart, you'll make it. I won't let you die."

Rosie, her voice was speaking to me: as she touched me, as she rubbed my chest, pushed hard on my stomach. But it was like a fading dream in a distant nightmare—she was not real.

"I want to die! Just let me die! I can't breathe. Just let me die!" I was screaming. I was crying.
"Then I'll be free! I want to be dead! I want to die!"

I know what I was feeling, the words they ring so clear, so true. Hey, I mean when you aren't on the winning side of life, death has got a whole lot more to offer.

I don't really remember much more. I must have puked a lot, screamed a lot, cried a lot. They carried me though it though—true friends I guess. They carried me through the night. Not like some French wench, who when I went down, bent down over the powder.

I woke up about thirty-five hours later. Rosie was there. The place was clean, way cleaner than I ever seen it before. She looked at me,

"I love you Stewart."

*   *   *

Now, I'm not going to bore you with the illicit details of the proceeding two or three weeks that occurred post that session with the Thai powder of passion. I'm not going to describe any further the body of my lovers, for I already have. I'm not going to reiterate the type of love that they individually made, for that has already been spoken of, as well. And, I'm not going to tell you of the *pong kow* experiences that continued on and on. For though all of the above certainly did have their high and low points, little can add to the basic definitions which have already been included in this text. Perhaps more than that it is late, and I do not wish my fingers which exist here over these typing keys to become forever frozen into this semi-circular, non-straight position. Anyway...

The time that came to pass went on as it does; lost in between the arms of two lovers. Well, three actually; if you count the Junk.

The love, physical eroticafication was continual and daily. The Junk was equally on. The drink, (better make that four loves), well, its placement in the intoxication overview was more than present, as well. Even the *ganga* touched my lips a time or three. In other words, I spent the next few weeks stoned, drunk, and fucking.

It was oblivion—one day faded into the next, one moment into its successor. The days, I would spend with Rosie, until she would fade off into the evening as the sunset fades into the twilight. The nights were lived in the arms of Patricia, until the morning sun found its way and placed its glow in my eyes.

Both were happy, the day and the night. Both were content, they had been embraced. I was stoned, so I really didn't give a fuck one direction or the other as to what was really going on in my life.

The sickness never hit too hard again. Somehow when you are in maximum overdrive it never has a chance to. Sure, I puked once or twice, had a bad moment or three but somehow the distance continued and blitzed replaced the yearning for creativity and the continual inward discussion of what was or wasn't my feelings for Rosie.

This period of time continued until the fury of the fire came home to me and burned its etching into my lost soul forever.

*   *   *

I was in my apartment, it was night—one of the few that I had not chosen to find my inebriated way to Patricia's. By this point I was no longer under the perpetual spell of the intoxicants of others but had found my own way to make the connection to the Junk filled night.

I had sat down, settled in. There were no lights on, illumination, however, found its way into my space from the radiation of the outside world. A world incidentally, I no longer cared much for. My mind was wondering as the deep distance of the powder was taking hold.

No, the smell of oil paints no longer occupied my apartment. Did I care about my lack of creativity? No. I look at the stereo, still in kicked over pieces on the floor. Does its disrupted state bother me? No.

No, nothing—no-thing any longer had any effect on me. I had reached the perfect yogic state. The degree of disinterest, the state of no desire that all wise men had spoken of since the beginning of man. The state I had sought in India, as a monk. The desire I had desired, as a yogi. Yes, it was all mine. I had reached *samadhi:* total and complete freedom. How easy it was, I should have seen it all along. The *soma* induced indifference.

A knock came upon my door. The silence of peace was shattered before my very field of enlightenment. I was disrupted. No, I did not want to answer the door.

To my unhappiness I had left it unlocked and in walked my sweet semi over weight *pong kow* pal, Patricia.

"I thought you had gone to see Rosie tonight."
"Who?"
"Don't be coy with me."

Coy, now there's a word I had not heard in many a moon.

"I know that you've been seeing her. I've smelled her perfume on your body and in your hair."
"At least she wears perfume."

I was in one of those do not disturb, don't fuck with me moods. And, it was let's play a battle of the words type of thing. Besides, I was stoned and did not desire this conversation to continue anyway.

It was Patricia who over the last few weeks I had occasionally argued with, something I hate to do. The Junk and the sex had kept my mind far enough into the mode of distance, concerning Rosie, to never have a disagreement and to never have to feel anything but love, spelled with a capital L, for her. Let me reword that, it was the Junk that gave me the distance to forget about Rosie's other doings when I was not with her. And it was her practiced intensity that kept the feeling of love boiling in my heart when we were together. Thus, no disagreements.

"I thought you'd gone to see her at her show."
"Her show?"
"Don't play stupid with me, Stewart. I know that you've gone to see that stupid show that she does. That's where you get you ideas for sex techniques, isn't it? Or does it just turn you on to watch her get fuck?"
"What the fuck are you talking about?"

To make a long story short, Patricia told me after the words went back and forth for a time, that Rosie was doing a nightly show at this one bar over by the Pat Pong.

Now, I don't know if you have ever felt it, but there is that feeling when you just do not want to move, but for all the world's stupid reasons, you must. Stoned and laid up, it took everything I had to get my body up: hit the shower, hit the Java—I wished I had some speed or some coke to put my move on, but there was none, only Junk. Finally, I hit the door outside.

It was like an avalanche falling upon my head, a catastrophe that I had to go and witness for myself. It was like impending death; watching it, as the knife come slowly towards you and deliberately slits your throat.

"So you're going to see her do her show."

Those words of Patricia's rang in my ears as I travelled in the direction of the said bar.

"Why was I doing it?" I kept thinking to myself. I'm in no mood to be out here in this scorching night heat of Bangkok. And, what kind of a show could Rosie be in anyway? Probably a strip show or something stupid like that.

I got to the Pat Pong. I never liked it there, very much. I mean all the bar girl hookers, trying to drag all the tourists into the bars and the nightclubs. They pull your arm, flash some ass, but come on it is all the same.

I never understood why Bangkok has such a reputation for its red-light district. I mean it is only a couple of blocks in length. I mean like, a lot of places in Europe are far more expansive.

I walked the crowded street. I was in a mood of intolerable impatience. I walked, as the whores called me in, as the tourists gawked and believed the lies of the ladies. I walked, and it all began to hit me. This was Rosie's home turf. Here, the Pot Pong, what Bangkok is noted for and to me the most disgusting section.

As I moved through the crowd thinking how I too had once upon a younger, far more foolish time had my way here on these streets—got pussy. Was I now being punished for being such a fool?

I realized that I had not come here to the Pat Pong for a long time. Yes, more than a long time. Was it intentional or just no time, maybe no reason? I hadn't even visited the semi good book store that exists among the glow of the neon. Rosie, why were you here?

My reflecting was interrupted, as I passed the front of one of the establishment. A big tall and buff Australian was yelling, screaming, and fighting his way into the gutters with this far smaller Thai man. My thought was, what a fool; for no matter how big and tough he thinks that he is, there are a lot more Thais here than Australians. He fought on, the other tourists looked on. I didn't even have a chance to yell a warning as a Thai knife, yielded by a far smaller Thai man, smaller in bodily size than the Australian, found its way into his back as he fell into the street. Australians always think they're badass. I never liked them anyway.

I kept walking, with little interest as to the previous on goings. I found my way to the club. Met at the door by three young Thai girls of pleasure, saying, *"Come in, see the show."* I felt like saying, *"Yeah baby, that's why I am here,"* but settled for telling the one who had attached herself to me,

"No, I don't need a new girlfriend. No, I wasn't German. And no, I did not wish to buy her a drink."

The confrontations continued, confrontation with want-a-be lovers and would be hostesses as I tried to make my way to the pay extra showplace theatre in the back of said premises and plant myself at the semi crowded bar awaiting to see if what Patricia had said was true.

The loud disco music blared on. The flashing lights moved and were reflected in the spinning dance hall disco sequined balls. Tourists filled the place and watched the semi naked to the fully naked girls do their thing.

No, Rosie couldn't do this. She has far too much class for it. I mean she even dresses nice.

The beat bounced on. The dancers, danced on. The tourists drank, yelled, and laid slobs upon the in-house babes, on and on. No, this wasn't my scene, not at all. Nothing like this ever had been. Me, I like the illusion, the chance.

With every dance there is another chance. This was far too clear-cut and simple for the melodrama that I choose to inhabit.

Rosie, though she may be a hooker, certainly could not do a show in a place like this.

What had been probably only about fifteen minutes and three greyhounds later. Fifteen minutes but what seemed to be hours, there came an announcement of the next show coming to town. I parried and decided to chill one more round down for the road. In doing so I would then be assured that Patricia had just made all of this shit up and Rosie was just out getting fucked by some unknown, unseen stranger. So, one more and I could go home; call up and yell at Patricia. Get stoned and wait for morning to roll around when I could once again visit the crib of Rosie.

Now, I really don't know the best way to put this into written form—for all memories seem to sink in their entanglements. But, I'm not going to bullshit you here, like some fucking great novelist would try to do. The show, the next one did come forward. Come forward and go on. The music played. Female dancers, danced.

As the progression progressed, out comes this lady in a veil. Her body covered only by a flimsy black see through negligee. Yes, I knew instantly, it was the body of Rosie.

It's hard to describe such moments in your life. Such moments when a bottle is smashed across your face. Like when a woman who you have really loved finds out all the things that you have told her are all lies and there is no way to make them truths. Or you find your wife of a hundred years in the arms of your best friend. It's like your dog dying. Or, an angry wind breaking the string on the kite that you really loved and you watch it blowing away—fading into the abyss.

The dance, danced on. The tourists yelled and screamed to, *"Fuck her, Fuck her."* The veiled woman went down on her knees and began giving one of the dancing Thai dudes head, both at the same time. His dick came up. Their bodies were moving and grooving: hers and theirs.

I wished with all my heart, all my soul that this was not happening. I believed that I even prayed for a moment to make it not be real—make it go away. But no, it did not go away. I wish I did not even have to write this as I sit here now. I wish the ending had been more poetic, more happy, more special, more macho, more something, more anything. I wish...

As they swayed, one thing led to another, as those kind of things tend to do. The dude went down on top of her, planted the pup home, caught a trim, and they fucked to the rhythm of the beat. First him on top, then her, then... He didn't even have a very proud pony.

There was another guy on stage and I couldn't figure out what he was going to do. He kept dancing. But then, the fucking combo. Rosie rolled on to her side. The other dude, not riding too proud either. I mean I wouldn't be out there flaunting it if I were packing so light. But he moved on down and came in through the backside. One front, one back. The crowd went fucking wild.

Maybe I had a tear in my eye, I don't know but I was out-a-Dodge. The whores tried to pull me in to clubs as I walked back down the Pat Pong. One grabbed on so tight and would not let me go, I yelled, *"Let me go you fucking whore!"* My comments turned more than a few tourists' heads. This place was unworthy of me.

I walked until I finally got a taxi and took it back to my apartment. Patricia was thankfully not there but she had so kindly left my front door wide open. *"Stupid bitch."*

I walked through the darken place. I kicked things over, threw things. Drank straight, long deep shots from a bottle of vodka. I even yelled occasionally until someone down stairs started banging on the walls. *"Fuck you,"* I shouted.

I had to get out but there was nowhere to go. Outside, all I found was heat that made me angrier. Rosie, I had to talk to Rosie. That *mutha' fucking son-of-a-bitch* whore, who had stolen my heart, led me on, while she was still fucking other people.

I was so mad when one taxi passed me by; I threw my bottle at his car. When he put it in reverse to talk shit, I told him to get out of the car I was going to fucking kill him. He rolled up his window and drove away fast. I kicked his door, as he sped away.

Finally, I got a taxi. I sat in the back: antsy, moving, drunk, and angry.

I was hurt. I was pissed. And, I knew it was my own entire fucking fault. But no matter whose fault it is, you want somebody else to blame.

I got to Rosie's apartment. She was not there.

In no mood to play any games, I kicked the locked front door open. I walked through the apartment looking for something that would make me angrier. Something that she had hidden from me: another man's name. Addresses, businesses cards, anything. I found nothing but in the process of looking I had trashed her place big time.

I saw the small Buddhist shrine mounted on the wall. I front kicked it. It sailed through the air. In my drunken state, I fell along with it. I lie there on the floor, the shrine, and the statue of the Buddha, lay there on the floor. I looked at it, face to face. I began to cry.

I cried for a long time. Mostly, as in all tears, I cried for what I was feeling. Not caring of or for the position of anyone else. And, tears they don't mean a god damn thing anyway.

The Buddha lay there in front of my crying eyes. I thought how I had retraced his steps in India; what now seemed like so long ago. *"The cause of all suffering is desire,"* he said. Yes, it is. As it was then, so is it now and will be in all times to come. My illusion of artificial *samadhi* faded.

I stood up. I picked up the Buddha. I put the pieces of the shrine back together as best as I could. I told them that I was sorry for any bad energy that I may have given them and hoped that I did not hurt them and asked for their forgiveness. All things, even the so-called inanimate, have feelings you know.

I then went and got a beer out of the refrigerator, drank it in one shot. Then I passed out.

Awakened! Yelling and screaming, Rosie had come home. I never have been one to enjoy being woken up. It always seems to put me in a bad mood.

"What have you done to my apartment?"
"What the fuck are you doing to me?"

Now, I could go on in the discourse of the transpiring sequence of events but your imagination would no doubt say the same words that were actually spoken. So, to dispense with the unnecessary wordiness, I will leave it at that—to your imagination.

Being yelled at, it pisses me off. And who in the fuck did she think that she was to have put my heart through the wringer.

All anger can ever do is escalate. I mean if the words kept being said and the flames keep being fuelled, the fire can go nowhere but up.

She said the wrong thing one too many times.

Slap! I backhanded her very hard across the face. She fell on the floor.

"You are nothing but a god damned whore! You could have been anything! But you are just another piece of fucking trash! You could not even stop being a whore for me! You will never be anything else! Fuck you!"
"Do you want me to call the police?"

She said that, as she lay there crying on the floor.

"Go ahead bitch. I'll just tell them that you're a fucking whore and didn't give me my monies worth. Besides, you don't even have a fucking telephone!"

She didn't say anything else.

I should have seen it all coming. I mean, I'm a worldly guy. I mean hey, I have been around. I spent my formative years growing up in the gutters of Hollywood, come on. And I should have known anger could only build. I have seen it so many times before. But learn my lesson, no I never studied.

There was a part of me: the violent part, the street kid part, the animal that just wanted to beat the shit out of her. But, I didn't.

"You will never be more than a fucking whore. I hope you die a violent death."

I spit on her. I kicked over a few more things and I was out the door.

Just turning the corner to come up the stairs was her downstairs neighbors.

"Hey, what's going on up there?"
"Fuck you."

He grabbed my arm. That was his mistake. I inside crescent kicked him—right across the face. He was down. He was out—rolling down the stairs.

I don't know what time it was that I left, but it was getting light by the time I made it home. My apartment was still a mess. I should have gotten a Thai maid. I threw a few thinks around, broke a precious art object or three and decided that was it.

I took my canvases. I rolled them. I tied them.

Eight o'clock, it had become eight o'clock in the A.M. I went outside, walked until I found a taxi. Drove back to the front of my building. Told the driver to wait.

Three loads, the fucking lazy driver wouldn't help. I put the paintings, folded and rolled as they were in the trunk. It is amazing how heavy painted canvases become.

He drove me to the cargo booking station at the airport. I wanted him to wait. He wanted an international fare. Finally, price discussed in his favour; he awaited my return.

Canvases booked—Bangkok to LAX. Though it was a fight to get the attendant to give me/sell me packing boxes of the size and shape needed. They were on their way. Picked up days later by a friend in need, a friend in deed, a friend demanding some payment for his service; L.A...

Up to the airline ticket desk. Return route, evening flight; Bangkok to London via Karachi.

My apartment, I packed what I could, packed what I thought I needed. Fuck the rest. The building manager, none too happy, I had a lease...

"Hey, you can keep my stereo. Go pick it up once I'm gone."

Yeah, I left. I left with the distant sunset over my shoulder. You know, like in all the old John Wayne Westerns. I left with no goodbyes. No one I wanted to say goodbye to. I was gone, never to touch the *pong kow* again. Gone, in search of that European excellence—of Italian women who do not shave their legs or under their arms. I love it natural... On my way to Italy via London, flight via Karachi. But that's all other stories.

*   *   *

I think it was then, Bangkok. I think it was there, Thailand; that I became hard—too hard to ever melt again.

Since then, I have gone back to Bangkok several times. I never saw Rosie again. I never really looked for her. Patricia died of AIDS. She started power popping the *pong kow* in her veins. The last time that I spoke with her on the phone, she had just escaped a Thai drug rehabilitation center. She was proud, had hooked with a dude, they broke out, and immediately got high. Sad, her passion killed her. But, most people, I guess, never really have a passion, so they just wouldn't understand...

Awh, Bangkok, where the dreams are so close at hand and the desires so fucking haveable. They'll all kill you in a second and never look back.

*　　*　　*

the day time it is for dreams
the night time it is for the screams
and life,
don't believe the lies,
it doesn't mean anything at all